Praise for

ONLY TO SLEEP:
A PHILIP MARLOWE NOVEL

"Osborne, an accomplished writer of fiction and nonfiction, has been asked to imagine a new case for Philip Marlowe and—have a smell from the barrel, all you gunsels and able grables—it *crackles*."
—*New York Times Book Review*

"*Only to Sleep* admirably sidesteps the pitfalls of Chandler-esque pastiche . . . in its place, a Marlowe we at once know, but have never met before. As much a meditation on aging and memory as it is a crime thriller."
—*Los Angeles Times*

"*Only to Sleep* is a story about age and regret and murder. About the American Dream. About the Mexican Dream. It's the kind of book where, when you read it, it turns the world to black and white for a half-hour afterward. It leaves you with the taste of rum and blood in your mouth. It hangs with you like a scar."
—*NPR*

"Whether you want a believably resurrected Chandler book or simply a good novel, this is for you."
—*Washington Times*

"Osborne succeeds brilliantly . . . [he] captures the dreamlike quality of the original Marlowe novels."
—*Washington Post*

"Absorbing . . . semi-exotic, lushly described . . . a fine way to leave an old fictional friend, taking at last a well-earned rest in the sun after having given readers decades of pleasure."
—*Wall Street Journal*

ONLY TO SLEEP

A PHILIP MARLOWE NOVEL

LAWRENCE OSBORNE

HOGARTH

LONDON / NEW YORK

Copyright © 2018 by Lawrence Osborne and Raymond Chandler Ltd.

All rights reserved.
Published in the United States by Hogarth, an imprint of the Crown Publishing Group, a division of Penguin Random House LLC, New York.
crownpublishing.com

Marlowe is a trademark of Raymond Chandler Ltd.
Philip Marlowe image rights registered 2017, Raymond Chandler Ltd.

HOGARTH is a trademark of the Random House Group Limited, and the H colophons are a trademark of Penguin Random House LLC.

Originally published in hardcover in the United States by Hogarth, an imprint of the Crown Publishing Group, a division of Penguin Random House LLC, New York, and in the United Kingdom by Hogarth UK, a division of Penguin Random House, UK, London, in 2018.

Library of Congress Cataloging-in-Publication Data
Name: Osborne, Lawrence, 1958- author.
Title: Only to sleep : a Philip Marlowe novel / Lawrence Osborne.
Description: First edition. | London ; New York : Hogarth, 2018.
Identifiers: LCCN 2018017511 | ISBN 9781524759612 (Hardcover) |
ISBN 9781524759629 (Trade paperback) | ISBN 9781524759636 (ebook)
Subjects: | BISAC: FICTION / Literary. | FICTION / Mystery &
Detective / General. | FICTION / Mystery & Detective / Hard-Boiled.
Classification: LCC PR6065.S23 O66 2018 | DDC 823/.914—dc23
LC record available at https://lccn.loc.gov/2018017511

ISBN 978-1-5247-5962-9
Ebook ISBN 978-1-5247-5963-6

Printed in the United States of America

Book design by Lauren Dong
Cover design by Michael Morris
Cover photograph by Nikola Borissov

1 3 5 7 9 10 8 6 4 2

First U.S. Paperback Edition

Ca tontemiquico ahnelli
Tinemico in tlpc

· It is not true
No it is not true
That we come to live on earth
We come here only to dream
We come only to sleep

—AZTEC SONG

ONLY TO SLEEP

ONE

J UST BELOW THE OLD SPANISH MISSION, A FEW MILES north of Ensenada in Baja, I have the house that I bought from Larry Danish in 1984. There I live as an old gumshoe or jelly bean should, with my middle-aged maid, Maria, and a stray dog rescued from the garbage. Out at sea, the porpoises that never sleep. La Misión had been Larry's exile for decades. He built a Spanish-style villa perched on the rocks within sight of the old La Fonda Hotel and Bar, where, it is rumored by the staff, the margarita was invented during Rita Hayworth's many fiestas at that same establishment. It doesn't matter if it isn't true. But I too had known La Fonda, La Misión's only hotel, for years. I used to drive down here in the '50s, when it was still beautiful, before the world was turned into a silo of unsatisfactory teenage fantasies and a garbage dumpster of schemes. Before the SunCor corporation littered the coast with golf resorts and there was any such thing as spring break in Rosarito Beach. Back then I'd go there to lie on a bed in a dark room and dry out. By the '70s, I was still drying out and no longer noticed whole decades passing in the night.

The cliffs of teddy bear cholla remain. The lonely hot roads in the interior and the little churches with their tin-painted *retablos* of car accidents and death by cancer. The Pacific with lines of kelp, chilling waves rolling in to a beach between rock headlands shrouded with mist and spray. This is what all of California once looked like. Close your eyes and wonder. I often do. How easy it was to destroy, easier than destroying a cherry cake with a plastic fork. All for a bit of tin.

But it's a good place for an old man. A sanctuary of clean wind and two hundred days of sun. On weekends I played the casinos in Ensenada. There was a bar there called Porfirio's, I think, which had a machine on the counter called El Electrucador. It was a kind of Van de Graaff generator with two finger pads. You put your fingers on the pads and the barman, with some noise and fuss, gave you a stiff shock. If you could withstand it, you got a free shot of mescal. I didn't need to get it free, but I got it free all the same. I figured the shocks were doing my intestines and hair roots some good. People said I looked much younger when I came back from my weekends. They said I looked "returned from the dead." At my age, I'll take any compliment.

We, the old guard, go to the terrace of La Fonda at night to eat its roast suckling pig and often stay there all day playing cards among ourselves under the palapas and running up our tabs. *Alive* is a relative word.

They play Los Tres Ases and Los Panchos tracks on the sound system, and there are some of us who can dream backward to the splendid years. There is still an occasional glimpse of the old times here, and maybe it's the last glimpse we'll ever enjoy. Has there ever in history been a time when four decades could turn everything upside down in such a conclusive way? I can remember the summer of 1950 in this very same place. Men in flannel suits and the women dressed like movie stars to go to the supermarket in the daytime. Thirty-eight years on—not a great amount of time when you think about it—the gentle sound of swing has given way to Guns N' Roses. Back then, the old Mexico was still there, hanging on to life with style. Pedro Infante was on the screens and Maria Félix was in the air. They were destroyed to make way for Madonna.

Then one day, after a low near-decade of sloth and decay and Ronald Reagan, two men from the Pacific Mutual insurance company walked into the terrace bar of La Fonda Hotel. They were dressed like undertakers and had sauntered down from the main road above the hotel, finding me seated alone with my pitcher of sangria and my silver-tipped cane as if they had known I would be there unaccompanied within sight of my home on the Baja cliffs. They knew which house it was, too, because their eyes rose to take it in, and they smiled with the small contempt of company men.

They'd heard I was retired, but a man they trusted in La Jolla had said I was the best that money couldn't buy. That was, of course, the best joke of the afternoon. They offered to buy me an early dinner and bared the teeth of friendly hyenas who have done their killing for the day. The older one held out a card that gave his name, Michael D. Kalb, and the other simply told me his: O'Kane. Kalb had at least twenty years over his colleague, but both of them were lean enough to carry the undertaker look. When I had put down the *habanero* and they had settled down into their chairs, the older one spoke with a voice that made me think of a father telling a bedtime tale to a child with attention-deficit problems.

He glanced with distaste at the Baja beach and his eyes were dead. Boys sat there under palapas, selling cattle skulls and lumps of floating kelp hacked out of the waves, yet it was clear that Kalb didn't know their world, or mine, and that he had probably never ventured so far south before. Was he surprised that the sun still shone so gently?

"It's a pleasure to meet you, Mr. Marlowe. Sandy and I weren't sure we'd be able to find you down here. You bought that house on the cliff?"

"It's called Danish Mansion. A lifetime of beating people up went into buying it."

They laughed, but there was surprisingly little sound.

"Let's get some margaritas," Kalb went on loudly. "I like the frosted glasses with the salt around the rim."

"They were invented at this hotel," I said. "Rita Hayworth used to come here. Margarita Hayworth."

I wondered who had recommended me. Years had gone by since I was last on a case, beating sidewalks in proper leather shoes, yet many of my former employers were probably still alive. Deirdre Gowan in Del Mar, ancient but able to remember my services; the Garland family whose daughter had gone missing in '79, and whose happiness I had restored. They were not yet ghosts.

"It's an easy job," the younger one said. "Did you ever meet an American called Donald Zinn down here in La Misión? They say he used to come to Mexico a lot."

I said I'd never heard of him.

"Surprising. But anyway, he was a developer with a lot of debt who died in a swimming accident in a place called Caleta de Campos in Michoacán last month. He had a policy with us and we have to pay the widow. The paperwork all checks out fine on the Mexican side."

"Except," said Kalb, "that it's not entirely fine with us."

"In what way?"

"Mr. Zinn had a policy with us for a number of years, and he had included his wife of about seven years. So there's nothing suspicious about recent events relative to the policy. But we understand he had been going to Caleta de Campos for a number of years and that he was not prone to doing risky or adventurous things that might endanger his health."

"Drugs, maybe," O'Kane said.

"What I'm trying to say is that there was no reason to increase his premiums or regard his policy as risky. Quite the opposite. Despite being profligate with his money, he was not considered a risk by our department. But with a death in Mexico, we never know what the circumstances really are."

"Suppose," the other chimed in, "he had committed suicide or even died in the course of committing a crime. Our liabilities wouldn't be entirely the same. The picture would change."

"Do you see, Mr. Marlowe? It's remarkably easy to bribe people down there here to alter facts on a death certificate. It happens all the time. Caleta is a small village on the coast, fairly remote. It's at least seventeen hundred miles south of the border. The embassy in Mexico City receives the report from the local police, the local coroner, and so on, and they rubber-stamp it before forwarding it to us. Most of these claims are not questioned. The insurance companies just pay out and they leave it at that. And yet we know fraud is going on. Well, maybe not fraud in this case. Maybe an embellishment of the truth to make Mr. Zinn look less responsible for his own demise than he might have been. What, for example, if he had been high on drugs at the time he was trying to swim across the bay at Caleta de Campos? I think that would change things."

"You'd have to pay out less?"

"Possibly. There's also the question of the cremation. He was cremated locally in Mexico, and very quickly. It's unusual to say the least. We've come to the conclusion that it might be worthwhile for us to take a second look at the file. We thought you might like to go down there and check it out for us."

"To where?"

"Well, he hung around in a number of places. As well as Caleta de Campos, he liked to big-game fish in Mazatlán. Perhaps we could get a better idea of what was going on the days leading up to his death."

They had with them an envelope, which was now laid upon the table.

"Here's some information on him. The widow is named Dolores Araya and she's still running the resort they built together near El Centro, out in the desert on the American side. You could go up and have a chat with her."

"I haven't accepted yet."

"You have a point there! Shall we have another round of margaritas?" Kalb said, slapping his hand on the counter. "I'm not saying it'll influence you. You'll only do it if you want to do it."

"That's what I'm thinking about."

The drinks arrived. I hadn't worked in ten years and I had

retired too late as it was. In those final days, I felt I had run out of courage rather than energy. Seventy-two isn't a bad age, but sixty-two is too old to be working. You are just impersonating the man you used to be. Retirement had seemed like the best way not to die, but the adrenaline had gone the day I threw in the towel and it never returned. You have your books and your movies, your daydreams and your moments in the sun, but none of those can save you any more than irony can.

I looked out now at the beach and felt as bored as I had the night before. The same old conversations of expats who were declining night by night on the terrace. The same gossip about neighbors and real estate deals and aging adultery and petty crime down the coast in Ensenada. The same overheightened indignations about things that didn't really matter. I realized then that I had never anticipated getting old or not being needed. I was suddenly flattered by the presence of these two men in slim black suits with their salty lips, even when Sandy said, "You're the best man for the job. We need someone inconspicuous."

Someone far and away over the hill, in other words.

His colleague assured me that it was nothing strenuous or physically risky. It would not be like the old days. I was too far gone to be a hero, and I wouldn't have to be one.

"We know you speak fluent Spanish, and that's the essential thing. You'd just be collecting some information for us. Would you like a couple of days to think about it?"

Kalb handed me his card and I was tempted to refuse it just to see the look in his eyes.

"I always decide on the spot, you know. It's a bad habit, but it's a habit."

"So?"

I knocked back the second margarita and rolled a coin in my head. It came out heads, and I always go with heads.

"Well, I could give it a try."

"Excellent," Kalb said, and there was a subtle relief in his tone. "I can set up a contract with my office tomorrow."

And he rattled off terms.

"You can make that three hundred a day expenses," I interrupted him. "I'd want to go to San Diego and see where and how Donald Zinn had spent his time, and then go to the resort and see Dolores Araya. Seeing the wife is always the fun part."

"Then we have an agreement?"

We shook hands then, and the two relaxed and pushed forward the envelope that lay before us. Inside were a sheaf of photographs of both Zinn and his wife, and the places they liked to frequent in happier days, including the Marius restaurant at the Méridien Hotel in San Diego. It was a portrait of a marriage on two hundred thousand a year and a marina house on Coronado Cays. They had been told that the wife no longer went to the house but they had the keys, which I could pick up from their office when I was in town. How they had obtained them, they didn't say.

"Is that legal, to go inside their house?" I said, now that I was on their little team.

"Old Donald had a mountain of debt, so the bank took the house and pretty much everything else. We came to an understanding with them. But no, it's not legal. So if you want to look at the house, you'll do it discreetly."

"So he was bankrupt?"

"Dry as a salted fish. We can't understand how he came to have so much money in the first place. Perhaps he never did."

"The con men with great hair are the best," I said, looking at the photographs.

He was good looking in his way, with hair that age had not thinned or otherwise fallen into disgrace. The eyes were full of torment, the eternal fear of being exposed and hunted. A San Diego pill, not quite in the first rank but blessed by the creator with a Roman nose. The clothes he wore were fine, with the heft of heavy cotton—I understood the attraction. Fragments of equally fine cars appeared in some shots.

"I get the picture," I said, putting the sheaf down. "He's dead but he's still living. If he's dead, maybe I should go meet his ghost. It'll be extra if I do."

"All right," Kalb said with his glacial grin.

I raised my empty glass and made a toast to Rita Hayworth, and they had no idea who she was.

AFTER THEY HAD left and as soon as the first stars had come out, a tolling bell began to echo from the hillsides above, and I let myself drift from the present backward in time. The sea became quiet. My cane rested between my legs. The lights of the lobster boats came on, and I took my solitary tequila straight up. After dusk I drove up the coast to clear my head, following the line of cliffs bristling with agaves. It was what I did every night, racing as far as the new American golf town of Real del Mar. Amid the coarse and treeless hillsides the

HQs of the Frisa Group and of Radar Communications stood in howling winds. It was, I supposed, where Zinn had been working behind the scenes.

When I returned to the house Maria was already asleep and the dog was roaming the beach alone, as I let him do. With an unwatered bourbon I lay sleepless in my bedroom, whose single window faced the sea and funneled its noise directly to my bed. I got three hours usually, but that night it was barely two. The electric lights on the beach went off at midnight, but the sand was bathed in a dim glow from the hotel terrace. Lobster fishermen stood with their baskets in front of a wind-guttered fire and I watched them for a long time, shaking with insomnia. There was, I thought, something calling to me from out in the dark.

It came from out in the tempest, even from the lights of the fishing boats a mile out at sea. You can be called to a last effort, a final heroic statement, because I doubt you call yourself to leave comforts and certainties for an open road. But the call is inside your own head. It's a sad summons from the depths of your own wasted past. You could call it the imperative to go out with full-tilt trumpets and gunshots instead of the quietly desperate sound of a hospital ventilator. Victory instead of defeat. You know that it will be the last time you ride out of the gates fully armed and that makes you more curious than you have ever been.

TWO

ONE DRY MORNING A FEW DAYS LATER I DROVE UP TO San Diego and checked into a little hotel I knew in Hillcrest that long ago used to be charming. Now, like all things, it had faded and was preserved merely by failure. I got a kick out of being near Balboa Park and the rattle of gang violence late at night. The barbarians were not only at the gates, but well and truly inside them, confident and getting bolder by the day. In the evening I made my way down to Casa de Pico on Juan Street in Old Town, where I could devour a few suizas to the sound of a mariachi band with their ponderous double basses and silver-embroidered sombreros. It was a sad scene but I liked it. Everything familiar has its merits, just like everything sad.

I got a little booze high that night and had to be escorted back to my car by the gentlemen of the establishment, who were also wearing spangled sombreros. I assured them that I could drive back to my hotel, which was not far. But in the end I had to sober up leaning on the hood and it was a while before I could drive at all. At the hotel I fell into bed and lay there fully clothed, full of demonic premonitions. It sometimes happened when I went back to the booze, and I went back to it as soon as I was alone in America and not with my housekeeper and regulars in Mexico. It was as if the lights went out and in the darkness I crawled about, secretly delighted and ravished. Drinkers never learn the antidote. Our way of surviving is just to succumb once in a while.

The following afternoon I went to the Méridien. Since the Zinns went there frequently I figured the staff there would remember them and be able to tell me something about them. Maybe they argued in public, maybe Zinn went there sometimes by himself and met associates. Everything happens in restaurants. The hotel stood on the Coronado side of the bay surrounded by landscaped gardens and pools upon which silent swans and teal sat as if tranquilized. Its terraces looked out over the downtown towers; below it, on the Coronado shore, other restaurants would light up at night, great glass cages flickering with candles and set on the beach. It was a maze of waterfalls, bubbling streams, and blue lagoons. The new world. The Marius restaurant, though, had no windows. It was intimate and slightly suffocating, a place for more secretive rendezvous, decorated with beige limestone floors and honey-glazed walls. The manager was surprisingly helpful. I showed him my photograph of the Zinns and asked if he could find a reservation the couple might have made. It turned out they had been in some months earlier, and he showed me the reservation himself. I asked if he remembered them.

"Monsieur Zinn?" he said. "He was a frequent guest. He came every week almost. They always ordered a Pomerol."

"A Pomerol?"

"Yes, sir."

"Was he a heavy tipper?"

"I cannot think of anyone who tipped more heavily, as you say."

"Did they ever have an argument in public?"

He said he had never seen one. They were very private, they always sat by the wall, and they were always alone. They liked the restaurant, one of the waiters told him, precisely because it had no windows.

"That's a curious reason to like a restaurant."

"People come here for the privacy."

"Did he ever meet anyone else here?"

"He came midweek sometimes and had lunch with gentlemen. Never ladies. Sometimes they left together."

"What kind of gentlemen?"

He shrugged.

"Gentlemen."

"No Able Grables?"

"Excuse me?"

I'd forgotten he was too young to understand the reference, and I had to laugh off the gaffe.

"I'm sorry, I mean girls. The loose kind. That's what we called them back in the day."

I walked around the absurd hotel afterward, thinking how it might suit a man like Donald Zinn and how much he must have liked it. I was trying to understand his world, but in reality I already knew it. There were hundreds of Donald Zinns trapped inside hundreds of similar lives. They were no different from the swans and teals imprisoned within the landscaped gardens. Except that Donald was a black swan.

After lunch in the hotel I drove down to his abandoned house.

Coronado Cays lay in a place called Silver Strand to the south of Coronado itself in the direction of Imperial Beach. It was a series of quaint villages with West Indian architecture built around an artificial lagoon. The townhouses had their own mooring docks and each one had a yacht parked outside. Zinn's included. There was a guard at the gate decked out in a white jacket and pith helmet, Bermuda-style, and the units had blue limestone shake roofs on chalk-white walls and arched Antiguan windows. There was a clubhouse with a gold-and-white-striped hip roof and a weather vane, and the Zinn residence was on a piece of the lagoon called Green Turtle.

Before their offices closed for the day, I stopped in at the Cays Homeowners Association and coolly asked how much a Green Turtle beauty might cost me. About three quarters of a million. It was useful to know. There was a lot of Japanese money pouring in, they admitted, and the Cays were the chicest address on the water now. Given how ugly it was, there was no reason to doubt it. I parked in front of the Zinn place and went up to his door. The insurance men had given me a key. A hand-fired tile set into the wall showed both his name and the number of the unit. I let myself in and found myself in a long front room hung with silk curtains with eighteenth-century indigo patterns. It was obvious that the people from the bank had been there and that they had done an inventory. There were little tags on some of the handsome antique pieces.

It was the house of a man both used to money and anxious not to lose it. I went upstairs and looked through the three bedrooms. On the mantelpieces were framed photographs of the couple, one at a polo field and another at a restaurant in Paris. Such are the interchangeable decors of the materially fortunate. The wardrobes were still packed with his splendid clothes. The velvet smoking jackets, the Huntsman suits, the shirts from Rome (or Horton Plaza). I sat in one of the velvet chairs, which seemed to match the jackets, and wandered through a bathroom with white shutters. It was as if they had walked out the day before and would be back for tea.

But it was all, of course, built on debt. That was the key fact about the Zinns: they borrowed and they never paid back. Paying back is for crumbs and heels. It's the art of mirrors.

MY LAST STOP was the offices of Zinn's company, Desert Blooms, in Del Mar. It lay on a street called Camino Real, filled with tree-shaded compounds and elegant developments, and all around it were the lush San Diego canyons bursting with flame vines. Del Mar was a favorite Mafia hangout because of the racetrack and the seafront hotels, and in the fifties at least, it had been a place where the *caporegimes* liked to play. I remembered it well, and not particularly fondly. I played a few blackjack tables there myself back in the day. But now it had moved up in the world, or down, depending on how you looked at it. I found the building where Desert Blooms was located and went up to the first floor. There, sure enough, were the glass doors with the company's logo, but behind them all was mothballed. The office had closed down, and rather recently as far as I could tell. It didn't mean that they were out of business, but they were no longer on Camino Real. A stack of sealed boxes stood on the former reception desk.

I took a few photos of the closed office and went back down to the street, where nothing awaited me and nothing was to be found. His widow must have wrapped up his affairs swiftly and sold everything that could be sold. She was a wonder of efficiency. Now I understood why Pacific Mutual had gotten the shivers, even though there was nothing they could put their finger on.

THREE

T HE NEXT DAY I DROVE OUT TO EL CENTRO, TWO HOURS
east on Interstate 8. I hoped to catch Dolores on the premises of her resort before dark came, but first I went out alone
to the Salvation Army house on the edge of the commercial
lettuce and radish fields where the border town peters out into
dust and haze. There, by the Salvation Army, a fairground
was in full swing in the spring heat, a Ferris wheel preparing for dusk and Mexicans in tall white Stetsons with their
girls on their arms. Two miles north of the border it was still
Mexico. It was ninety-seven in the shade and there was no
shade. A warm day, you might say, at the end of spring, or the
beginning of hell, or else in the middle of the Anza-Borrego.

I bought a sugared churro and wandered about at the edge
of this hidden world, feeling young for the first time in years.
It happens like that, and sometimes in a single moment. You
are no longer seventy-two years old. The ocotillos bloomed
red, their flowers like stiff paper cups, and the mesquites were
filled with gracklings, as if they were the first signs of a new
lease on life: an old man in a ragged cowboy hat blinked
at them and wondered if he had a year left after all. A year,
maybe even two. I looked at my watch and saw that it was past
three o'clock.

An hour later, I drove past the Southern Pacific freight yard and the edge of the ghetto beyond, past miles of light industrial warehouses, faded silos, and unused lots of desert scrub. In the area called Northside, gang insignia were sprayed onto the curbsides, *Nuestra Familia* and *La M*. The dark jacarandas and billboards loomed over the roads selling the virtues of Farmers Insurance and Sharma Homes. North of the city lay the human wilderness of Brawley and Calipatria. I knew the Salton Sea all too well and I doubted whether it, too, had changed much in eleven years. How much could a place called Slab City change for the better? The dread was eternal. Back then I'd spent blissful days at Bombay Beach and Durmid under those burned-coke mountains interviewing dead people. One day I'd go back as a tourist, but not in this lifetime.

A mile from the road was the site of the Palm Dunes Resort, and it was indeed an oasis of transplanted palms. The work crews had walked off one fine day—so it seemed— leaving the cement mixers and the hoes in place, and now there were only the adobe bungalows sitting in their glades of ornamental saguaros and the pools emptied of water but still glittering with art deco mosaics. The sand had blown in with the winds and silted up the public spaces, leaving ridges against the locked doors and the windowsills. I got out of the car and walked around. A security man tried to intervene but I charmed him off with some loose Spanish. He even told me how long the site had been shut down. And what about *el patron*, I asked. He shrugged and said he had no idea. He was a developer who had run out of money for his Dune Palms.

"What about the señora?"

"Señora Zinn?"

"She's still here, isn't she?"

He looked up with greater wariness into my old eyes that he didn't know and my gringo sneer.

"How come you speak Spanish anyway?"

"I retired there."

"Mexico?"

I said it didn't concern him, I just needed to know if Señora Zinn was in her office that afternoon.

"*Claro que si.*"

I gave him a tip and didn't ask permission to walk up to the gate and peer inside. He watched me go, and said nothing. The place was like a graveyard in Jericho. The sun drenched the empty pool and the Imperial palms felt aloofly out of place now. So the San Diego rich had not come after all.

I went through the shaded reception area and into the office, where the air-conditioning was the first relief in hours. It looked as if the company had fired everyone but kept the air-con on as a refusal to admit defeat. I called out Dolores's name and then called it again until something stirred. She was alone, and when she appeared through one of the glass doors, surprised and a little perturbed, I recognized her at once from the photographs the insurance company had given me. I stepped forward to announce my name, my hopeless mission: Philip Marlowe, so recently uplifted from retirement. I flinched as her eyes took me in, and something took me aback. The eyes were not closed against me, they were open and inquisitive—but not too much so. She had the level interest in something new that a leopard has. While it decides whether you can be killed or not, its eyes are remarkably gentle and serene.

She was petite, her features small and carefully drawn, and about thirty or so, if I were to hazard a guess. Mexican or half at least, and much more attractive than the picture had suggested. She wore a black skirt and jacket, with a thick white cotton shirt underneath, and the shoulder pads were dramatic, a little too much so. The style of that terrible age. Her face, though, was perfectly made up, like a flawless arrangement of ikebana. She seemed dressed for a date in the middle of nowhere, and I wondered if she dressed like that every day, or whether she was expecting someone. The bars of an old song suddenly went through my mind, "Begin the Beguine." The music of the '40s, to which my hips are still attuned. I wondered for a moment what it would be like to sweep her off her feet and dance. I would never know.

I took off the straw hat I was wearing and asked her if she was Mrs. Zinn. She sized me up and ascertained in a heartbeat that I had come alone and that the hat doffing was a condolence as well as a greeting. At that moment, those same eyes changed their mood and burned violet with a quiet fury that even her elegant makeup couldn't mask. It occurred to me that she had been waiting for me all along, and that everything was an act until now. I explained I had come at the behest of the insurance company that had paid out the dividend.

"Are you here for a reason?"

"It's their reason, not mine. Your husband had a policy with them."

"You don't need to tell me that. I know all about them."

"They're sweet people when you see their emotional side."

"Shall we go into my office?"

"We can stay here, there's no one around. Looks like you're closing shop. Is that the case?"

"It might be."

She offered me one of the dusty office chairs and I sat, feeling a little tired in the legs and parched.

Noticing which, she said, "Drink?"

"I'll take water."

"I have some old rum if you'd like it."

In the end we didn't touch it.

There was a large window behind her, and inside its frame the palm trees stood still in a shrill light nevertheless dimmed and rendered golden by slowly falling sand. So this was the dream of the Zinns until her husband had washed up on the beach at Caleta de Campos. The hysteria of it was still written on her face. I said I was sorry about all that, and she took it in stride. The very fact that I was there cast a long shadow of doubt upon her grief and therefore made my presence insulting.

"You look a little old to be running around doing work like this," she said once she had seated herself behind the only desk in the room. "Aren't you an old-timer?"

"Actually I'm retired," I began. "But an old friend asked me to do this. You know how sore the insurance companies get when they have to pay out money to widows. Don't take it personally. I just have to ask the usual questions."

Her gaze went straight to the heart of my fog-bound decrepitude. I felt myself wilt for a moment and then remembered—

as an afterthought doused in sadness—that I was too old now to ignore her eyes' brilliant light and spring back at her.

"Go ahead," she drawled. "I have an hour before dinner in El Centro."

An hour: she made it sound like a small eternity. It would be a vacuum that she would have to fill with pleasantries, whereas for me it was an opening into a short wonderland that would be the best hour of the year. She was at her ease now, more languid, as if these moods came upon her suddenly and out of nowhere, and there was more humor at the corners of the mouth. She settled down, like a snake finding its spot in the sun.

So it went.

My questions were hardly original. I asked her about her husband and their marriage. They had been together seven years; they owned a real estate business that had run, as far as I could see (and contrary to her denials), into trouble. They had no children; her parents lived in Mazatlán, They went to San Diego once a week to eat at the places that aspiring rich people liked to frequent, places like Mille Fleurs in Rancho Santa Fe or the very Marius I had just visited. The latter was their favorite venue for a Friday night romantic dinner. Donald had been seventy-one at his death, twice her age. But only a little younger than me, I thought with a moment's envy. He had gotten to lie next to this beauty night after night like Gandhi among his Nereids, indifferent to the dangers of his good fortune.

The payout to her had been two million dollars. And therefore arose the question as to what she intended to do with it. But that couldn't be asked directly.

"You must be sad here," I said. "The place you built with Donald. Is that why you're closing it down?"

"Of course it is. Would you stay on if you were me?"

"Surely not."

"It's like living in a ghost house. I could make it work if I had the spirit. But I don't. I'm exhausted."

"So did you sell it?"

"I did, Mr. Marlowe. I sold it to a company called Dragon Tower. They'll probably pull everything down and start again. But as for that, I really don't know."

"I'm sorry to hear it."

"Donald would have been devastated. But I have to be practical."

"Don't we all? I don't blame you for that. There always comes a time to move on, as they say."

"I guess I've come to that time. Would you like to have a look at the property? I know you're going to ask anyway."

She seemed about to be ingratiating, stepping toward the door. I laughed, admitted that it was so, and we went outside, our shoulders almost touching for a moment. The heat blinded me for an instant and I felt my balance sliding. Out of the momentary darkness came the sly agreeability of a smile. She was an Able Grable on the make, flirtatious to an old wreck and therefore faking it. But still. We walked around the resort in a blistering late-afternoon wind, and I leaned heavily on my cane. My lips were suddenly dried out and puckered, and my eyes as well. The water remaining in the pool quivered and rippled, and between the deck chairs the sand had begun to accumulate. The ruin was well advanced, but it had not yet triumphed. The pool bar still had bottles of Stolichnaya under plastic, and the unit windows still had their curtains. Yet at the edge of the property, the sand was making more serious inroads. The incoming company was paying to keep the sprinklers on so the lawns wouldn't die. And to think, she said, that Donald had laid those lawns down himself. With a shovel and trowel, I thought, with no help from Mexicans?

"Did you go to Mexico to deal with the body?" I asked, thinking to take her out of her stride. But she took it in with that glassy coolness she always seemed to marshal.

"I did. It was a terrible thing. He was a good swimmer, so I don't see how it could have happened. Did you ever see a drowned person?"

"Plenty. They look kind of peaceful."

"He didn't look peaceful at all."

"You know, it can happen—tides and all that. It doesn't matter if they're strong swimmers."

"The police there said he had been drinking heavily and that maybe there were some drugs on the beach. You know he had marijuana in his blood?"

"They told me."

"I should have gone with him on that trip. But a fishing trip is a man's trip. He and his friends always went to Mazatlán for marlin."

It was jauntily said and I liked the way there was no reproach in it: she hadn't minded that he did his own things in his own time.

"Is that where you met him?"

"I was a waitress at one of the clubs."

"Always the way," I murmured.

"There's nothing wrong with it. Men marry waitresses all the time. They ought to."

The look was not altogether contemptuous. We came to the large gardens that they had spent a fortune to create on desert soil and which Dragon Towers was now paying to lubricate. Tall datura shaded a path made out of seashells.

"Where are Donald's ashes now?" I asked.

"I have them here. Would you like to see them?"

"Not especially."

She winced and her sarcasm failed a little.

I said, "I'm sorry he died that way, by the way."

It couldn't have happened to a more ambiguous guy, I thought.

"I suppose you're thinking we were having problems," she went on, however. We walked under the datura shade and its sweet smell changed the atmosphere between us. I felt the old rhythm of charm, the beginning of a dance in which I was no longer an adept partner. "Well, we were, but that doesn't mean anything. Everyone in business goes through periods when there are problems. I'm sure you've been through times like that yourself."

"I'm going through one now, as a matter of fact."

"Then you understand. It was just temporary."

Pacific Mutual had gone through the numbers, and the failure of the resort had to be reckoned in the millions. The affable Donald had borrowed ten times more than he could ever pay back, and he had done so purely on the back of the same allure that had seduced a young waitress into a life very different from the one which she already knew. In the pictures I had seen he was the most dapper man in any room, at least in the middle strata of the beautiful and chic. But other than that he was a local boy with fingernails filled with El Centro dirt. I was glad I'd never met him. I would have hated him as well as envying him his wife. But many of his earlier developments had failed, and each time he had managed to escape utter ruin. He was one of those beguilers whom I have known all my life. An old-school snake charmer whose blood was immune to venom. He had ventures all over Mexico because there the law was weaker and he could get away with more: it's an old story and Dolores knew it just as well as I did. Then one night, at three in the morning, tanked up on tequila and dope, he went for a late-night swim off the wild beach of Caleta de Campos and a riptide or a jellyfish ended his improbable streak of luck. Adios, *pendejo.* By a slip of fate he had left his young widow provided for, and there was nothing wrong with that in my book. There was a lot right with it.

Our little tour ended with a gate that opened out into the open desert and its layers of arroyos glittering with yellow cholla flowers. The oppressive mountains at the horizon gave it its foreboding and its sense of endless time, yielding nothing.

"After you've wrapped up here, Dolores, where next?"

"I haven't decided yet. Maybe I'll go home."

"It's never a bad idea. What do you think Donald would have wanted?"

"To go home, no question."

But then where was home, exactly? She didn't seem like

a person who had one or even wanted one. She had that in her eyes: the shiftiness of the vagrant, the ever-moving pupil that reminds you of an apple bobbing in dirty water. But now she seemed impatient to have done with me, and I felt myself being ushered very subtly back toward the gates. To slow the momentum, I asked:

"I was just curious about one thing."

"Yes?"

Her eyes were suddenly no longer hostile or apprehensive.

"I wanted to know what you loved most about Donald. I mean, what drew you to him when you first met him?"

She paused and thought on the question. She finally said that one night at the Crocodilo Club, a man in a burgundy velvet smoking jacket came in with two girls and asked for the cigar collection. It was a cliché, she said, but it was such a confident cliché that it had made her laugh. What was wrong with clichés, anyway? They served their purpose. That was Donald. A cliché in a smoking jacket, but with a big, sentimental heart and terrible blue eyes.

"Oh, were his eyes blue?"

"Blue as they come. Blue as a little boy's."

We walked back to the main office, and the wind came through the sad arches with a brutal heat and we covered our faces. She didn't invite me in and I was in no position to insist. My brief allotment of her time was up. My cane held me up in the gusts and sand flew into my eyes as she saw me to the gate.

"I don't know why they asked you to come," she said as she stayed in the shade and I ventured back out into the glare.

"The reports were all filed correctly with the police down in Caleta de Campos. The embassy looked over the papers and they said—"

"They're just doing their job, Dolores. It's nothing personal."

"I'd prefer it if it was."

I shook her hand and there was a dutiful farewell, a question about whether I could see her again, and suddenly she was calling out to the guard to help me to the car. *"No me necesita,"* I called back to him, and he hung back. She watched me crawl back to my rental, and her hand was lifted to her eyes to protect them and to see better the plates. I felt that she was memorizing them. In a week, maybe two, she would be gone, and Pacific Mutual would have no idea where she would be gone to. A figure of quiet elegance and melancholy as she stood in the shade of her ruined gate, her hand raised and her lips pursed. Glad to be rid of me, no doubt, and protective of the urn standing somewhere in her empty rooms. *"Hasta la vuelta,"* I thought, but didn't say.

IT WAS DUSK by the time I got to the Kon Tiki Motel on Adams Avenue in El Centro. The motel boasted a neon green and yellow palm that leaned out into the street and sputtered as night came down. There was a gravel courtyard filled with the beaten-down cars of the Okies who came to work in the lettuce fields in Imperial Valley. The owners were Chinese. Their daughter played a violin in the back room, something romantic and Russian, and their life went on behind a drawn curtain. I went up to the second floor, opened the door, flung my bag onto the bed, then locked the door behind me. The room doubled as a temporary sauna. I turned on the AC and the walls shuddered, and after a half hour it began to cool.

I had a bottle of rye with me and poured a shot into a paper cup and drank it on my back on the bed. It was fine enough in its way and I dare say it calmed me down. It always does. I laid my cane next to me and dozed for an hour. At some point the violin stopped and I seemed to rouse, but it was a false start: I was still sleeping. A dark-red moon hung above the ragged manzanita trees and one could see nothing by its light. When I did wake, though, it was morning and I was still in my dust-heavy clothes of the day before. I hadn't eaten in twelve hours and had begun to wither inside. Seventy-two years old, I thought and still disheveled at 6 a.m.

I went to the diner on Adams and ordered chimichangas with heavy cream and *agua de Jamaica*. The wide avenue beyond the window had no passeggiatas; it was empty but for whirls of grit blown in the desert wind. And yet its ghost-world luminosity came through the same window and fell upon my hands as they lay next to the sugar shaker. A fossil alone in his little rock bed, curled up as if ready for the eons. As sidelined as the old Pacific Electric Red Cars that used to plow their way across West Hollywood. I wondered who was in the huge finned machines rumbling through the heat of Adams, passing under the palms, the windows darkened, the mariachi turned up: assassins unable to find their early-morning prey. In twenty years, or even thirty, it had changed only outwardly. I had sat at a window like this in 1971 and watched the sugar trucks go by and wondered why my hands looked so old before their time. At that time, it was the machinery of homicides that consumed my mind. But the years of retirement had drawn me away to simpler pursuits: whiskey collecting, amateur telescopes, and porpoise watching, and I had lost the habit a little. Now the panoramas outside whatever window I was sitting by filled me with gentle interest, and little more.

All the same, now that I had met the real Mrs. Zinn eye-to-eye, I was more interested than I had been the day before. A beautiful fraud is like the merging of two elements that combine to make something far more formidable than the merely beautiful and the merely fraudulent. One of those can always bring you back to life.

It was afterward, as I drove down to the police precinct, where I knew one of the detectives—we'd worked together on a case a decade earlier—that I wondered if I should have just driven home and forgotten about the whole thing. But there was the money, which I needed, despite what I'd said to the goons from Pacific Mutual. And the feeling that comes with not being entirely useless to the world. So I drove on. The precinct was a low sixties building a few blocks from Imperial Avenue with no air-con in the lobby and numerous photographs on the walls of law enforcement heroes going back to the twenties, policemen posed on the sideboards of their cars with tommy guns and tilted brims. Spiders crawled over the ceiling as if unconcerned by interruptions, and in the cells a few vagrants slept on their sides through the heat.

Bonhoeffer was the man I knew. His face looked down from those same photos, but now it was made more complex and tormented by the passing of years. We had worked together on a case by the Salton Sea in which three people had been cut up and sunk inside suitcases, three dead people who had turned out to be drug runners. I had been hired by the wife of one of the corpses to find him, and find him I did. But not in the way she had hoped. Bonhoeffer had been the calmer of us two in those days. He never got into fights and he never raised his voice. The aura of fear that surrounded him—and of which he was not entirely aware—made such vulgarities improbable, as did his way of looking at you as if one eye were closed when it was not. He suggested we go for a drive somewhere with takeout coffees.

"You look a little rough," he said in the car. "Should you be out and about like this?"

"I'll be all right."

"Yeah?"

"It's my choice after all."

"That's the worst part," he said.

It was a blue day again, and the desert shone a powdered-chalk white under the promise of a cloudless sky. We came to the Yuha Cutoff and Signal Road. Mount Signal was where all the cocaine from Mexico came in. Bonhoeffer was in a buoyant mood and he seemed fatter than when I had last seen him. He was a charlatan, I thought, trapped in the body of an honest cop. It must have been a difficult lifelong act. But in the end the act had become a reality, and I supposed that that meant he was not a charlatan after all.

When we had gotten out and were in the stillness of the desert, sipping our coffees, I asked him if he had ever come across Donald Zinn.

He flinched a little, and then looked away in the way that people do when they are in fact not thinking about far-off things at all.

"Well, the Zinns are an old family here. Donald was the flamboyant one. Sure I came across him. He was drunk driving so many times I forget."

"He never had any convictions, though?"

"Let's say it's why we're out here having this chat in the middle of nowhere. Donald was one of our characters. I wouldn't say he was a bastard through and through. I rather like his wife. I feel sorry for her, and maybe you feel the same. I just have a hard time believing he's dead. I feel like if he came to the moment of death he'd talk his way out of it. He really would. Death would roll over and give him a contract disfavorable to hell."

"That's quite a talent."

"Yes, sir, it is. But as for you, Philip, you really shouldn't be out here chasing after smoke and mirrors. Not at your age. What are they offering you?"

"A fair pile."

"You're not going to Mexico, are you?"

"I live there already."

"But now you've come out of retirement?"

He leaned against the car and placed his hand on the hood. As far as the eye could see, the shining cholla spines formed a kind of flowering minefield that undulated over the arroyos. A faint whiff of ammonia came on the wind.

"I wouldn't go down there," he said quietly, "unless it's just to go home. I heard you got a house near La Misión. Is that true?"

"Been there awhile now."

"It's not the same world up here, for sure. You did well to get out. Do you remember that body we fished out of the Salton Sea in '79? Turned out it was an Italian in the real estate line. I hear he got into a shouting match with Donald in a bar in El Centro. It's just a rumor."

Perhaps he had a point, I thought.

"You have a good life, Philip. You're too old to knock people out. Stay down there and go fishing. They can't be offering you that much. Or maybe you're just bored."

"There's that. I never thought retirement would be so sad."

"What's sad about doing what you want?"

"Maybe I'm just not old enough yet. There are some mornings—I just want to get in my car and disappear on the road. It's like that. It's a stupid thing to explain."

"Then don't," his eyes said, and they were merry enough.

"Don't you have a girl down there? You always used to have one."

"Used to."

"Well, that's a sorry thing for a start."

"You know, I was married once, but the condition doesn't agree with me. It makes me unstable."

"That's the thing," he growled.

Is it? I thought. Was it something everyone knew then, a doom that lay around every connubial corner?

I spent the next few days in San Diego thinking over what he had told me and making a few calls to people in the real estate business whose names Bonhoeffer had given me. None of them played ball, however. It was as if word had gotten out that Donald had gone on the lam, a has-been gumshoe was

33

after him, and it wasn't worth their time to cooperate. But I had known all along that, sooner or later, I would have to take a plane to Mazatlán. And I didn't mind the idea at all. It was a place for vacations and a Carnival that was said to be one of the biggest in the world. I'd always wanted to see it. That, and a stronger sun and some dolphin watching. It must have been the late '50s or early '60s since I had last been there. Years can turn a place upside down; or worse, turn it right side up.

FOUR

So it was that i flew down to mazatlán with a crocodile bag and a matching skin wallet filled with Pacific Mutual cash, ten days before Carnival. In that same bag I had packed my slightly quaint devices—a small radio transmitter with bugging devices, a pair of opera glasses, and a subminiature Minox camera. The opera glasses I always took with me on jobs because they proved inconspicuous to bystanders while observing people from afar. I also carried the cane that has been my constant servant since I broke a foot in 1977, and inside which slept a Japanese blade that a master smith had custom made for me in Tokyo. A *shikomizue* inspired by all the Zatoichi films I had watched in the '60s. For Zatoichi, a weapon for the blind; for me, the weapon of old age, of impotent slyness.

In the town, the streets were already filled with yellow balloons and piñatas, with music and little girls, and there was a small box of superior cigars in the cantinas. I found a hotel among the ruined houses that had been bombed during the Revolution and never repaired, went up with my single bag and my flask, and pulled open the shutters.

One last fling of the dice, I was thinking, and there wasn't a better place in which to sink or swim. To me it was "the old country," the last magical place on earth, the world's navel.

I had already researched the car I would rent, the restaurants I would hit, the bars I would soak up. My weight would go up, and the gods who determine mortal beauty would laugh into their hands. But Mazatlán was smiling on the Tropic of Cancer.

Along the Malecón, the hustlers were in a good mood, and from the same viewpoint I could see karsts green as jade and shaped like stalactites. A new world, bathed in the light of the past. But as I'd driven in from the airport I'd noticed the walls covered with a repetitive and grave graffiti: *Fuera los corruptos!* Yet they would never be thrown out, the corruptibles.

Although it hadn't been a long flight from San Diego, I took a bath and went through the numbers I had obtained for Donald's cronies at the Marlin Sports Club. After Bonhoeffer's leads dried up, I called up some of my old real estate friends in California and they delivered the goods. Donaldo's friends were all Americans, with a few rich Mexicans thrown in for good luck. Some of these fine upstanding citizens had known him for many years, and prior investigations by the company had revealed two or three that might prove to be more useful than the others. Such a person, for example, was Edward Delahanty.

Delahanty owned a hotel in town called the Rubio, a bustling and slippery place at night, and it was there I went to meet him when the sun had come down over the Malecón and the mood had altered for the night.

He was the same age as Donald, and he liked to sit at his

bar at all hours keeping an eye on the transactions. I took his coif for a wig at once, but it turned out not to be so. He had it spun finely like gossamer at a salon in town and then dyed to the color of an eggplant after a fair amount of stir frying. You could tell that to his own eye it was a vast improvement over nature, whereas of course the opposite was true. It was eight o'clock and he was in a palm-motif shirt with silver bangles on his wrists and a bauble watch. Profits turned nicely on the Tropic. Many of the deep-sea sportfishermen stayed there and played out their Hemingway twilight days among shakers and girls in perilous heels, overwhelmed by back hair and bellies but happy in their cups.

I had called Delahanty two days before and he was expecting me, though my appearance didn't seem to impress him for all the glory of my vintage tie.

"You look like a spook," he said at once, glancing at my cane, and shook my hand without getting up. "Do people still wear ties down here?"

"Mexicans do."

"Let's have a drink. I recommend the Rubicon. It's our house cocktail. Get it, Rubi-con?"

"Is it red, too?"

"It's grapefruit juice with mescal and some sugary stuff. Rosa, *dos Rubicones!*"

I said, as men do in such situations, "Quite a place you have here."

But he made a face.

"It's a shadow of its former glory. Mazatlán has gone downhill these days—it's become friendly to *families.*"

"So I've noticed."

"Were you here twenty years ago?"

"Make it thirty. Yes, I remember all right."

"Ah, a dinosaur—the best kind! Donald and I used to go to the Camino Real Hotel and eat at the Chiquita Banana. It was his favorite place."

The drinks came, alarmingly iced, violently red, and served in brandy glasses.

"*Arriba, abajo, al centro,*" he cried, lifting his and touching mine. "*Pa dentro!*"

The mescal hit me sweetly and I rediscovered a touch of vigor for the evening.

"So you came to ask about Donald?" Delahanty leaned back in his chair. "I heard about his death. At first I thought a shark got him. But now they say he drowned after a few drinks on the beach. I say it's not the worst death. Not by a long shot."

"When was he last in Mazatlán?"

"That same week. He always came here for a bit of fishing, then went down the coast."

"What did he go down the coast for?"

"What does anyone go down there for? Girls and dope. He wasn't a pure-at-heart surfer. The surfers go to Faro de Bucerías. Caleta is where you go for Acapulco Gold. They grow it in the hills. Plus you can anchor a yacht there."

"So he didn't drive?"

"Drive? He took a yacht there. Him and his friend Dennis Black. They always went without the wives. Black, I believe, is in Manzanillo right now. That's where he berths in the winter."

"So they went down together."

"Probably, it was an annual tradition. I've heard a lot about those trips on the Black yacht. I wonder if Donald ever told his wife."

"I wonder if she asked."

"Never met her myself. Even though she's from here. Is she pretty?"

"Too good for the likes of us."

He smiled.

"That's what I like to hear. Glad Donald didn't let the side down. Now I suppose she's rich. Gringos have their uses."

He turned the glass in his hand and stared into the bloody ice mush.

"It's all fair," I said. "We're paying for their time, aren't we?"

"I guess we are at that."

"They wouldn't be with us otherwise."

"Ain't that the truth."

It didn't seem to bother him, however.

"I'll tell you what," he went on. "You should go down to the Marlin Club and ask after Black. They'll know where he is. You can probably find him somewhere down on the coast. He spends the whole winter there going from port to port. There's a group of them spend the season on their yachts like that. We call them the Wild Bunch. It's a terrific movie, have you seen it?"

"Sure I have."

"They probably trade in dope with the local dealers and sell in the cities when they come back. It's been rumored. But all I do is sit all day at my bar, which means I don't know as much as I think I do."

"I think you know plenty. And I'd like to buy you ten more drinks. Or will nine do? Waiter—"

"My kinda guy," he bawled.

I asked him to tell me what he thought of Donald, and he could be honest since the man was dead.

"Donald? The most generous man in the world. He ruined himself being so generous. He loved all the parasites hanging on to him. I've seen him spend thousands in one night on people he'd never met before. If it's an illness, perhaps they have a name for it?"

"I'll look it up later tonight."

"Personally, I think he wanted to die by the end. You get to be too old, that's all, and when you get to that point you suddenly let go of all your scruples about dying and sprint to the end any way you can."

"Is that what he did?"

"Maybe. A man goes swimming in the middle of the night in a dangerous spot of sea—probably after a liter of tequila."

"But it sounds," I said, "like he had a kind of second life down here. Maybe no one up north knew about it and he preferred it that way."

"Maybe he did."

He smiled a second time, and his eyes deliberately caught mine and held them for a moment: pure mirth. Every man has the idea of a second life somewhere, or a parallel one. For how many years did I not have the same idea in mind? A place where I could don a fake mustache and become Don Filippo, a place where no taxes were owed and no memories stuck to your pelt.

"Tell me, Philip, are you treating this as a vacation? I would if I were you. You won't find anything in Caleta de Campos. The *federales* down there are good old boys—you know them. Bribe them and let them talk and talk, it won't do you any good. Donald knew what he was doing."

"What do you think he was doing?"

"I think he'd had enough. What about you—have you had enough? Or would you like a girl for the night. I can arrange a favor."

"I'm out of the combat zone now," I said, brushing his suggestion off with a wave of the hand. "But thanks anyway."

"Have another Rubicon, then. Rosa, *dos Rubicones*."

I thought I might as well enjoy it. As he said, I was on vacation. It was not like the philanderings of my work journeys of yore. My pilot light had long been blown out and I liked it better that way because now there was no need for it to be on all the time. My eye did not react like mercury to the sudden appearance of women; I had cooled. I looked around me in a more calculating way. This was Donald's secret extramarital world. These little dance floors with available women swinging themselves to *cumbia*, to El Tropicombo tunes, drinks with paper parasols and maraschinos, smoke from other lungs. Nights in town and on the high seas with the Wild Bunch. I was beginning to become better acquainted with Donald Zinn, a man who was already dead.

"You would have liked El Donaldo," Delahanty went on, reading me in some way. "You'd have had a good time together. Maybe even had some people in common. You never know. He could tell good jokes."

In the underworld, then.

"I haven't been in those circles for a while," I said. "I got my fill of it back then. I live for fishing and restaurants now."

"It's a shame about Donald. Now I think about it, I remember one of his jokes. It goes like this: a tortoise goes to the police after he was mugged by a bunch of snails. The tortoise police ask him what happened. But the tortoise is confused. I can't remember, he says, it all happened so quickly—"

He slammed down his glass and his eyes went apoplectic before the inevitable burst of laughter.

"*La chingada!*"

"I wonder if he made it up."

I downed my Rubicon and it had curiously little effect on me.

"So are you going to Caleta de Campos to follow the trail? They told me that the body was cremated down there on the spot. Is that true? I wonder how it goes when you wash up dead on the beach. Don't they identify you and notify the embassy and then ship you home?"

"Not always, it seems. Maybe there were reasons. It's a small settlement, I hear—they're a bit cut off from the outside world."

"He sure picked his spot, didn't he?"

"It looks that way," I said.

Delahanty glanced up at the wall for a moment, at a clock whose numerals were made of little bottles.

"I wonder where he is now?" he smiled. It was a question that actually might have had an answer.

———

THE NEXT MORNING I took a taxi out to the Marlin Club. It lay on the water north of the Hotel Playa toward the marina, an informal clubhouse for a private sportfishing fleet moored inside the marina and owned by an American called Ronnie Sugar. Sugar himself was there, fat and yet muscular enough at the same time to man a rod on a boat's fighting chair. Now land bound, his monstrous form was settled into a deck chair in the sun, facing two shadowy islands that rose from the sea in front of us, and the hand that shaded his eyes was covered with Aztec rings. He wanted to know who I was, and I had to charm him into eventually admitting that he knew Mr. Black. Fortunately, my name meant nothing to him.

"And what do you want with Dennis?"

My shadow lay across him because he had not invited me to sit, and so there was a touch of the Diogenes about him. Would he ask me to move out of the way of his sun?

"Delahanty suggested you might know where he is now. I'm from the insurance company, but it has nothing to do with him."

"So it's about Zinn?"

"Is he a well-known character down there?"

"You'll find him in minutes. He's not the hiding kind. But if I were you I'd be careful around him. I don't allow him on my boats these days."

"Why is that?"

"He gets a little frisky with the machete. There's a good way to kill big fish and a bad way. You know what I mean? Now, if you don't mind—"

"There was one more thing, though. Did you know Zinn well?"

He took this with weary equanimity.

"He came fishing on my boats, if that's what you mean. I didn't ever ban him for getting drunk. He was a bad fisherman, but he liked the social life. You're going to ask me what I knew about him. Nothing. I think he had some real estate deals on the coast, but it was none of my business. No, his wife never came with him. He was a cokehead, but I've seen worse. It rubs you a little the wrong way on a guy that age. He never grew up. I called him a bastard because he once chewed out one of my boat hands in a nasty way. I don't let anyone do that. He had a nasty side. Many of them do."

"It sounds to me like he was *meshuga* a bit. Was he?"

His face clouded and he wondered if I was making fun of him.

"You mean was he crazy?"

"Yeah, not playing with a full deck."

"You could say that. *Meshuga!* You talk like you were still twenty-five, Marlowe. Is that Ice Age slang?"

"Old habits and all that."

"No, I like it. And that's a funky old suit you're wearing, old sport. When did you get that made? D-day?"

I looked down at my own duds and wondered myself. It must have been the wide chalk stripes and the high-waisted look, but at least without a hint of zoot. I always dressed conservatively. Old pieces from Hart Schaffner & Marx out of New York, but maybe he was right and I had let the years flow under my bridge without noticing.

"If it fits, it doesn't look bad."

"Still, it's 1988, hombre."

"How about Zinn? Did he wear the latest stuff?"

"He was pretty sharp. Sharper than you. But I can see you're a nicer person."

"So he flipped his wig from time to time," I said. "It's not a capital offense. We all do that, don't we?"

"No, we don't. He's a bastard and I couldn't care less about him. But I don't want to have lunch with you, Mr. Marlowe. I want you to be on your way. Black is in Puerto Vallarta now, if you want to know. As you're aware, it's on the coast, so it's on your way. If you find him, you don't say I told you. Or I'll come down there and kill you myself."

IN THE BRILLIANT noon light I went down to the Hotel Playa and had lunch near the beach, enchiladas suizas with white sauce and a bottle of Baja white wine. This was the world in which Donald Zinn moved in his spare time, but so far there had not been any expressions of real sorrow about his passing from the earth. He seemed to have struck them as a grown-up adolescent whose true character rested in a permanent state of obscurity. Halfway through the bottle, I asked the hotel to call a place called the Conchas Chinas in Puerto Vallarta, an establishment named for the village where it was located, and reserve me a room for a couple of nights. It was little more than a four-hour drive in my rental car, and I wanted to get there that same evening. Instinct moved me. Black was there and I wanted to corner him before I arrived in Caleta de Campos.

In the end, it was a longer drive.

The heat had gotten to me and the long, straight road in its white dust played on my nerves. As always, there were the iron shacks arranged in grids where the children come racing toward the car to hunt for coins. The sesuvium that gave the slums the false color of gardens.

But in the green and rolling hills I stopped among the usual abandoned buildings and the meadows filled with poppies and lay down for a while with heaviness in my mouth. Between milpas of maize tall, forked saguaros rose into a dark-blue atmosphere, and I slept with my silver-tipped cane beside me in the hot beaten-down grass and dreamed of the bodies I had seen a lifetime earlier. Bodies sometimes sprawled in fields a little like this one, or else slumped at bars where they had been shot in the temple. The unfortunate can die anywhere, and they often looked like children asleep, with faces that I had known when they were living.

FIVE

P UERTO VALLARTA PACKED A LOT OF NOSTALGIA FOR
me as I grew older and the town became younger in appearance. Its golden age was really around 1964, the time of
Night of the Iguana, and many were the golden days I had
spent there then. Now all the people I had once known had
either died or moved on. South of the town lay the village of
Conchas Chinas, where that film was shot, its old hotels sitting on top of cliffs that plunged down into a petrol-blue sea.
It was in 1958, I believe, that I came here with Mona Kotzen,
a girl I picked up in Los Angeles while working on the Smith-
son case. She must have been twenty-three at that time, a
marvel I met in Whitley Heights while talking to her father,
and I carried her off in my godly chariot to the rocky coves
where the waves beat on the precipices all night long. What
had we said to each other during those nights? They must
have been important and beautiful things, but now I couldn't
remember what they had been. The words, like Mona, had
melted into the ether. But the hotel and the owner, whom I
had befriended years before, was still there. Danny Combes,
with colorful-motif shirts and a broken nose, and the bright
eyes of the ones who will never die easily.

I took a room overlooking the cove and the little private

beach, the cliffs covered with shining organ pipe cactus from where local boys launched themselves into the air for a lovely moment before shooting downward into the surf with knives between their teeth, like kingfishers, purely for the pleasure of guests. They had done that in the old days, too. Marimba wafted up from the hotel bar. The sun set behind spear-like agaves as I had dinner on my balcony.

The rich have their secretive mansions around Puerto Vallarta and down the coast in places like Costa Careyes and Tenacatita. Houses as beautiful as anything in Provence and set into a coast not unlike the Côte d'Azur. The owners come up to Puerto to eat at the elegant restaurants, even though it's a long drive each way. Many of them stayed the night at Conchas Chinas.

It was an hour's work to ascertain that Black's yacht was moored at the Paradiso marina in Nuevo Vallarta north of the center, and that he came into town every night with his girl to have dinner on the rooftop terrace of Chez Elena. At nine I walked up to the marina in a navy blazer with brass buttons in the hopes of catching him on the yacht, and the boys there told me that there was in fact a small party going on in the *Deep Blue Devil* that evening. They pointed out the yacht and I walked around the marina with my cane, struggling a little because the arthritic cramps that sometimes plagued me had returned. When I was opposite the gangplank I saw that it was not a party at all but just a middle-aged man with a Mexican girl and a boat's captain of sorts in a cream-colored uniform. The middle-aged man—Black, I assumed—had a sunburned pirate's face with a ridiculous dyed goatee and eyebrows painted on with a calligrapher's brush. The man fighting the signs of aging always has a touch of sinister vaudeville about him. But his threads were impeccable. The three of them were playing cards at a glass table with a bottle of Jav's rum and listening to Bob Dylan. Black was in a V-necked Yale sweater with a white shirt underneath and crisp whites with dark-blue Sperry boat shoes. There was, in fact, something lifted out of the *Official Preppy Handbook* about him, as if Lisa Birnbach had had something like his figure in mind as she instructed our decade on how to do the look right. It wasn't what I had expected, but then I wasn't sure what I was expecting in the first place. The scene was sedate and gentlemanly, with an air of ancient reasonableness. There was even a liquor cabinet stationed politely by the table, with shakers and long mixing spoons and obviously expensive glassware. The three looked up together as I appeared at the foot of their gangplank, and out of nowhere, summoned by a general sense of alarm, a butler appeared and called down in a Filipino accent, "Yes, sir?"

The girl tittered, perhaps as I was a little overdressed for the occasion, and the middle-aged man whom I took to be Black rose from his chair and stepped to the edge of the boat to get a better look at me. Suddenly he smiled.

"Ahoy there. Do we know you?"

I made my case, making it as affably as I could, and pretended to be a friend of Zinn's rather than someone investigating him. Again, my name did not ring any rusty bells.

Black turned to his companions.

"He says he's a friend of Donald's."

The girl was skeptical. "Really?"

Black turned back to me.

"You came here all alone without calling? That's rather odd of you. Personally I don't mind. Would you care to come aboard for a drink?"

The butler helped me up the gangplank, my legs feeling the stress. It was a handsome yacht, a multimillion-dollar affair, a Knight & Carver Riviera, if I wasn't mistaken. When I was seated with them, Black asked the butler to make me a Campari and soda since that was what they were drinking, and he asked me the inevitable questions about myself and Zinn—did we know each other from San Diego? I said I'd known him from years ago and since I happened to be on my way to Acapulco I thought I'd find out how he died. It had saddened me to hear the news.

"Same for us all," he sighed. "I heard while I was in Manzanillo. You can imagine—"

"So you weren't traveling together?"

"What an idea. No, he was on his own as far as I know. It's quite a wild place, Caleta. It was one of Donald's hideouts. Of course we drop anchor there ourselves sometimes, usually in the winter. It's a nice little bay and the bars on the beach are sweet. You can swim in from the yacht."

"Then I wonder how he got there last July?"

"Oh, he hitched a ride on one of the yachts going down there. It's a big party scene at this time of year. They swim in from the yachts all boozed up—well, you can see how accidents happen."

"It seems a little foolish."

The girl was eyeing me up, cool and unconvinced. I had the feeling she had seen through me at once. The eyes were a dark Castilian green, like coins sunk in old water.

"You're driving?" Black said cheerfully. "Splendid way to go. I should try it myself someday. They say the roads at night are getting violent, though. There are certain stretches you should stay off past nine o'clock."

"Oh?"

"Kidnappings and all that. It's a disagreeable fact of life. Stick to daytime driving, if I were you."

"Even dusk," the girl finally said.

Her name was Elvira, the accent American as it turned out.

"At first," I said, "I thought Donald had been kidnapped. I admit it was the first thing that sprang to mind. He had enough enemies down there, I suspect, they could easily have kidnapped him and held him for some ransom. I wouldn't have been surprised at all. It's such a pity—he was a lovely man. Wasn't he, Elvira?"

"He was a rake, let's face it."

Black laughed.

"They're so cruel when we're dead. When we're alive, too, come to think of it. But he *was* a bit of a rake. So was I once upon a time. How about you, Mr. Marlowe?"

"You've got me there."

"It's the blind judging the blind, then. There's nothing wrong with being a bit of a rake. It didn't get him killed at least."

But that, I thought, was an open question.

"Unfortunately, Marlowe, a fair number of aging white men die here every year. It's a sort of yearly harvest. When you consider why they're here, it's not surprising. They come for a thrill and they find it. That's all I can say."

"It's pretty dismal," I lied.

"It's what it is. You have to wonder if it's what they're hoping for deep down. You have to die somewhere, so why not here? I'd say it's a pretty fine place to die, all things considered."

"I can't think of anywhere more beautiful. Capri, maybe. But who can afford to die there?"

He lifted his glass to toast the departed Zinn.

"To Donald, may he rake the Elysian Fields!"

The butler served some small tortas and I asked about the American scene on the coast. The world of tanned men in big-shouldered jackets with a taste for cigars, of marlin hunters and whore mongerers on the lam on the cancerous Tropic.

"They come and go," Black went on. "We all need something in this world, we all come from places where we can't get them. I wouldn't live in the United States if you paid me by the minute. Can you imagine ending up in a hospital there? Can you imagine trying to pay for a night of *sensualidad*? After a certain point you get tired of angry adolescents. You get tired of five hours' sleep a night and endless white noise. Then you run for the border. When I see the thousands running in the opposite direction, I am reminded of certain facts of human nature that are not encouraging. But you have to make your peace with the world and find your place to die. In the meantime, you can just push the envelope a little."

"I don't know—no matter how much you push the envelope it'll still be stationary."

"Still," he went on in a different tone, "you seem awfully curious about our mutual friend. And are you just, as they say, passing through?"

"That's about the long and short of it."

I glanced at my watch—the classic move—and uttered a ritual sigh. Time to be moving on. I stirred and the butler sprang forward to help me up. But Black waved him away for a moment.

"We're sailing down to Manzanillo ourselves," he said calmly. "You're welcome to join us if you like. We can even sail on past Caleta—what do you think?"

There was a note of threat in the invitation, like a clenched hand inside a very pretty glove.

"Thank you for your offer, but I don't like yachts—I get claustrophobia."

"Very well. Sam, could you help Mr. Marlowe down the gangplank? It looks like that stick of his will get in the way."

I gave them an old-fashioned bow and I was aware suddenly of the sweat glistening all over my face and the effect it must be giving in the light of the sickly yellow lamps on the deck.

"You're shaking," Black said as the butler ushered me toward the gangplank. "I admit our Sam makes a strong Campari and soda. But even so—"

"Are you all right?" the girl asked.

"I'm on my way," I answered, and wished them a *hasta la vuelta*.

I picked up my cane as if simultaneously sweeping a cape and got back onto my weary pegs. My exit was grand enough.

On terra firma the butler gave me an anxious look.

"Do you know how to get back to town?" he asked.

But the question seemed to conceal a different one—it was a curious coded warning to leave as quickly as possible and to not come back. I wanted to thank him for it and in the end he walked me back to the car.

"He's a curious guy, your boss," I said on the way. "Does he eat live scorpions for breakfast? I was just curious."

"Just croissants."

"I'm taken aback. Are you really sailing to Manzanillo tomorrow?"

"No, sir."

"Well, give them all my fond regards."

"And you have a safe trip, sir."

As it went I stayed another night at the Conchas Chinas and during the day I sniffed around in town asking after Donald Zinn. But he was the man-who-never-was. Come dusk I took my drink on my balcony and watched the boys plunge into the cove below like little Tarzans, and I reflected that they must be the grandchildren of the boys I had first seen here in 1958. Time was cruel, and it was me who had changed for the worse. It was my hands that shook as they reached for the salt pot. Maybe Black was right and the Tropic was the honeypot that sucked all the flies in and drowned them in honey, and for that matter Zinn and I were not so different. Men on the lam, pathetic crumbs with long pasts worth forgetting. Zinn had just found his exit and a way to provide for his young widow: it wasn't so dishonorable when you thought about it twice.

SIX

STOPPED AT MIDDAY IN CUYUTLÁN TO BUY SOME BOT-tled water in the day market. The streets there lit up in shocking colors with flame vines and coral trees. It was on the sea, the wind fine and salted, and along high curbs in front of lime-white houses, women with Aztec faces stood selling *gorditas* stuffed with shredded and half-burned coconut and baskets of the same red coral tree petals. Already, it was a dif-ferent place from Puerto Vallarta. I felt blinded and refreshed at the same time, my cane clattering on the cobbles and my senses fumbling. The sacred Colima volcano loomed nearby, and the voices in the streets whispered in Nahuatl. In the shade of the volcano, then. Coconut groves cast an other-worldly cool over the ground below them, through which little streams made their way down to the sea.

Farther along, the road became tortuous, dipping up and down through forest, and at least once I stopped the car to let a tarantula make its way across the road in the same way you would stop for an old lady. Mountains rolled down to the coast, where the breakers smashed against beaches piled with driftwood, and their slopes were covered with ghostly shaving brush trees with open flowers.

As the sun neared its zenith I came into view of Caleta

de Campos. It lay against the wild hills with a beauty created purely by neglect. It was a somnolent village built around two separate bays connected by a few dirt paths, and where these paths converged there was a small hotel called Los Arcos. But on the slopes pitching down to the sea the houses seemed to be mostly abandoned. Behind the hotel was a village square and cantina, and beyond that the road and the mountains shining with cactus. It was a settlement of hundreds at most, maybe only dozens, and under the neon glare of midday there was no one to be seen either way.

I parked the car under a tree by the hotel and went into the lobby. A fan stirred the air and a girl was asleep at the desk, her head on folded arms. I wasn't sure how to wake her up. Finally I coughed. She stirred, opened one eye without shame, and said, "*Buenas.*"

I asked for a room with a sea view.

"*No hay.*"

"All right, a room with no sea view."

She gave me the key and let me take the room myself.

Once there, I threw open the shutters. There was a fine sea view. Then I walked back down to the lobby and found that she was asleep again.

From the front door of the hotel, a dirt path led down to the ruined villas and the main beach. I took it. Soon a harbor wall came into view with the words *Cerveza Corona* painted in white letters along its length. To the left, the beach curved away toward a headland covered with more ruined houses, and along it stood palapas with hammocks. The bay was sheltered, the water calm. I made my way down the slope onto the beach, took off my shoes, and wandered along the surf. The whole place seemed to be under a sleep-inducing spell. A path led up to the headland through a mass of low-lying cactus. So this was where Donald had met his maker. The palapas were, no doubt, where he had had his late-night parties over the years. I went back to them and chose a hammock. No one came out to take my order. Half an hour later I walked along the harbor wall to the end. When I got there I found an old man fishing by himself on the seaward side. I realized then that he had been watching me all along.

I sat on the wall under the shade of my own straw hat and we stared into the water together. Eventually I asked him why there weren't any yachts in the bay that day.

"They come and go," he said.

"No Americans this week?"

"They come and go."

Now, on the headland, I could see a group of three soldiers sitting on a piece of wall with their weapons stacked next to them. There was a drugs checkpoint on the road that ran right past Caleta de Campos. An old man fishing every day, I thought, must see everything day by day. I decided to make myself a friend. A shared cigarette later, his name was on my lips: Nestor. A great name for an old man of the sea.

He didn't put down his rod or turn to me when he said, a few moments later, "Are you looking for someone?"

"Do I look like I am?"

"Yes, sir, you do."

"Well, I'm sorry to hear that."

"You speak good Spanish."

"I'm a good mimic."

The sun was now so hot that my mind began to lose its

coherence. Even the sea wind couldn't hold it together, and so I gave myself another minute before I went back to the palapas. I asked him who he thought I was looking for. That got a chuckle out of him. I was asking *him*?

"There was a drowning here in the summer," I said. "Do you remember that?"

He said there was one every year, sometimes two.

"But that American—do you remember him?"

"The old one?"

"Yes."

"I remember him. He came every year. He used to swim across the bay."

"So he was a good swimmer?"

"He was good for his age."

Then, I said, it was strange that he had drowned.

"It was at night," Nestor said. "No one could figure out why he was swimming at night, though. Maybe he was high."

"Does everyone get high here?"

"The Americans do. They can buy marijuana anywhere they like."

There was a slow drawl to him, and a gleam of truth, that quality that cannot be faked by even the cleverest man.

I spent the rest of the afternoon at the palapas observing the pattern in all things. The old men who came down to fish and stayed all day on the harbor wall with their mescal. the little boys with buckets wading through the estuary looking for crabs. At five the radios started up and the kitchens opened for *sopa de mariscos* in tin bowls. The friendly women who ran them came down the dirt paths to enjoy the sunset. The best thing was to get into the swing of it, become a temporary familiar face, and order a lot of drinks. It was Pacific Mutual's time and money as far as I was concerned, and I'd be just as happy to waste a few days here, then go back to the land of gringos and report a dead end. But at the same time I would soon have to go to the police at the *delegación* and get their story. It would be a fanciful one and probably untrue, but I would have to get it anyway.

It was Saturday and that night there was a fiesta in the square. By the time I got back to Los Arcos the mariachi were already in full flow and the square was full. I went down there alone to watch the *rechulos* in their cowboy hats and pointed boots, dancing with their girls, and I found that the speakers set up in the square were taller than me and their sound made the whole village shake. I would have danced if my legs could have taken me, but all I could do was watch and wait. There's no sadness greater than that of a small village in the mountains where everyone is dancing in a square without you. I thought I heard a few guns going off as the boys got warmed up with mescal, but there was nothing menacing about it. On the contrary, it was a comfort. There was a bar with iced *michelada* beer, and I downed one as the sun dissolved and the dark outlines of the mountains became ominous. Soon only the brightness of the moonlit sea could countervail the firecrackers and the lanterns swinging from the wires around the square. Down by the road I found the *federales* and showed them my ID and said I would like if possible to ask about the American who had drowned seven months earlier. They were surprisingly polite and cooperative.

They said they would call down to the police station in the town along the coast, Lázaro Cárdenas, and that I could talk to someone the following morning if I so desired. I did so desire. Someone would come up in the morning and I could talk it over with him. Any drowning victim would be taken to the morgue in Lázaro, and it was the authorities there who would have processed the case. They were mild mannered and gracious, perhaps because of the festivities nearby and the quietness of the road that night, and they assured me they would keep an eye over me during my stay in Caleta. That night, after the fiesta had died down, I heard seabirds screaming above the cliffs and the sound of music coming from the palapas. And as I sat by the window I heard women shouting out of sight. It was a sound of joy and disorder and alcohol seething in human bodies. In the middle of the bay, quietly unannounced, a large yacht had swung into view with all its lights on.

SEVEN

I WAS TOO TIRED TO GO DOWN THAT NIGHT, AND IN-
stead I slept early and got up likewise. As I was taking a
pot of *café de olla* on the porch of the hotel, the promised
policeman appeared on foot, in civilian dress and coolly elegant in an open white shirt. His name was Homeros Nervos,
a fifty-something detective from Lázaro, a man of smooth
cheeks and faint aromas (some brut I didn't recognize even
after years of acquainting myself with scents) and sober al-
ligator shoes that didn't seem inappropriate on a detective at
the beginning of a working day. He simply walked up to the
porch and asked if I was the Mr. Marlowe who had asked to
see a detective the previous evening. I asked him if he'd like
something to eat. He spoke in English, and he spoke it as well
as I spoke his language, so we settled on that.

"No, I'm all right. I might take a coffee with you, though."

He joined me at the table and we found ourselves close together in that wonderful early-morning shade, with the wind
fresh off the sea.

There wasn't a cloud in the sky that day.

"You've come a long way," he began.

I explained everything to him without altering any of the
details. It was best to be honest.

"I see," he said.

"I just wanted to verify the story, as it were. It says on the certificate that Zinn drowned in the bay."

"That's correct. We did the autopsy in Lázaro."

His eyes were level and the color of freshly turned earth.

"What were the circumstances?"

"As far as we could see, he came in from a yacht moored in the bay. It must have been in the middle of the night, but the body wasn't discovered until the early morning. It had washed up on the beach."

I asked him what Zinn had been wearing. Nervos smiled at this and it was not just at the trivial memory of Zinn's costume in death.

"It's funny you should ask. He was in shorts and a linen shirt. It's possible he just fell off the boat in the night and drowned. He had been drinking heavily—there was a lot of alcohol in his blood, anyway."

"Why does everyone say he was swimming?"

"Who says so?"

But now that I thought of it, it was merely an assumption. So he maybe wasn't swimming, I thought.

"How much alcohol did he have in his system?"

"More than enough to knock him out. You're going to ask what the people on the yacht said. But when we got here in the morning there was no yacht. It had slipped away the same night."

It was half-true, and the smile held steady for a few moments and then melted away. There is an art to the mask, and he had practiced it long and hard until it was perfect. I asked him what the yacht's name had been, and he admitted that no one knew or could remember. It had flown a Mexican flag, but no one had known the people on it. Had the passengers, I asked, come onto the beach for dinner? He said that the palapa owners claimed that they had not.

He went on: "But unknown boats show up here all the time. I wouldn't say it was unusual."

"And you couldn't trace the yacht the following day?"

Wearisome, the persistent foreigner: Nervos stretched a little.

"We put out a search, but it came up with nothing. As you can see," he motioned with his hand toward the road, "we're busy with other matters. So we never found it. We have no idea who was on it at the time or who it belonged to."

"But Señor Zinn must have known them."

"Indeed he must have. But it's too late to find them now. I had a feeling—well, let's say that I had the feeling that the locals here knew them. But they're too frightened to tell us anything. They knew Señor Zinn quite well, but his circle of people—they'd rather not get involved."

"I had a feeling that would be the case. Do you think Señor Zinn was dealing drugs with the men in the hills?"

"Probably not. But I couldn't say. I think myself he was just a good-time boy who fell off a boat and died. The owners panicked and vanished. You can see it from their point of view."

"They ran from the scene of an accident. I can understand it. But then, they were not friends of his, were they?"

"I suppose not."

He turned his mild eyes on me and there was a great distance in them, as if we had walked away in opposite directions from one moment to the next.

"I also have to say," I went on, "that it was curious that the authorities here decided to cremate the body on the spot. Didn't you contact his wife and ask her what she wanted to do?"

"Who says we didn't? Of course we contacted her. She said the best thing would be to cremate him in Lázaro. It's a huge expense to fly a body to the United States. We confirmed the identity ourselves and sent the papers to the embassy."

It was extraordinary, but I said nothing—not even my eyelids moved.

"So she was all right with it? She didn't fly down to identify the body?"

"Again, I never said she didn't. She did indeed. She identified him in the morgue and we proceeded from there."

"I guess she must have been very upset."

"You can imagine. She stayed at the same hotel you're staying at here. Didn't you know that?"

"She didn't say anything."

"Ah, so you've met. A very pretty woman, wouldn't you say?"

And the distance in his eyes suddenly disappeared.

"I would say, yes. Too pretty for Donald Zinn probably. Normally it's dangerous having one of those."

"That's what I thought at the time, too. We know how it goes. I hear he had a rather large insurance premium on his head. It almost seems a cliché—but human nature doesn't vary much."

"No, Nervos, it doesn't."

I wondered which room Dolores had stayed in. He said that she'd wanted to stay close to where her beloved Donald had died. But she had probably had other reasons of a more practical nature.

"How long was she here?" I asked.

He stretched out his legs and eyed the cluster of tanagers that had come down to investigate the churros standing in a glass jar on our table. I wondered if he knew about the hummingbird god, Huitzilopochtli, or how Aztec warriors were believed to be reincarnated as the little birds. He watched them warily in any case, even though they are the most harmless animals ever evolved to torment breakfast tables. He said she'd been there for a week while matters were wrapped up with the body, and that she had been the model of somber propriety. She had signed all the necessary papers and authorized the cremation. She had taken possession of the ID that had been found on the body—yes, he had carried it with him even in the water—and which they had used to finger his name in the first place.

"So they found his ID on him?"

I smiled a little too brazenly, and perhaps he was momentarily offended.

"That's the way it was," he drawled. "Convenient, but true all the same. It's not me who decides how people fall into the water!"

It was a scene to imagine in the morgue: Dolores standing

over the bloated body of her husband trying to be cold and functional as she issued a yes to the question about his identity. Few further questions had been asked. Old white men dying on vacation or business were too common to fret about.

And the widow? She had gone back alone to California with the ashes.

"I felt rather bad for her," Nervos said. "I took her to the airport in Guadalajara myself. She said almost nothing the whole time. The paperwork went on for a while and she took it well, but she never asked me any inconvenient questions. I was quite surprised by that. I thought at the time she must have been in shock and that was all there was to it."

"It must have been an ordeal, all right."

Nervos gave me a look that at first seemed understanding but which, when I lingered over it, felt like contempt. But it was not a contempt that could be overtly spoken—it hung back in the shadows formed by the corners of his handsome mouth.

"Well," he said then, "I suppose that wraps it up for you. Are you going to stay on for a beach holiday? You can't find a better spot than this. Just don't go swimming in the bay. I hear there's a shark patrolling the waters right now. A tiger."

"I'll stay on dry land. I always do."

He slapped his thighs and the tanagers suddenly dispersed.

"You have a great job," he said brightly. "I envy you. Maybe that's what I'll do when I've retired. Get paid to sit on a beach."

"It's a con if you ask me. Thank you for coming up to see me. If I need anything more—"

"Just call me. But I don't think you will. This was one

of the more straightforward cases we've dealt with in recent years. I just feel bad for the people of Caleta. The gossip about things like this can damage their business. I've noticed the place is a little quieter since Señor Zinn's death."

Some men seem to materialize and dematerialize out of nowhere. Nervos was one of them. The shimmer of his lies was fine and pleasing, but beneath this surface lay all the knowledge and suspicion that he would never reveal to a man like me. So we are forced to read the puzzling codes that other men devise for us. I resented it—who wouldn't. But then, I had expected nothing else. It was Dolores who was the greater operator. She had acted well and picked up a life-defining fortune.

EIGHT

I T WAS BY THEN ONLY NINE O'CLOCK. WITH THE DAY ahead of me, I decided to take the same walk along the harbor wall back to the palapas, where I was hoping to see old Nestor fishing. He was. Before us the bay held at its center the newly arrived yacht, a large Broward flying an American flag, and a faint music traveled across the water to us from its decks, where two white women sunned themselves in visors. Nestor stood in exactly the same spot with his bucket of bait, and as I sat down on the sea wall beside him, he asked me if I had slept badly or well.

"I stayed up all night. I couldn't remember the words to 'Little Rabbit Foo Foo.'"

He said it was the ghosts in all the houses. He, too, had slept badly, and so did everyone else. Many dealers had been executed in the ruins, on the headlands, on the lonely tracks going up into the hills. They were shot by other dealers or by the *federales* themselves, who were free to do so if no one saw them. The bodies showed up in the basements of the abandoned houses or in the long grass fully exposed to the sun. Telltale clouds of butterflies marked the spots. The whole place had a stench of casual death. Across it lay a web of gossip and fear and rumor, and the wise ones kept their peace with themselves. The only way to break into this web was by means of a quiet *propina*.

I made our conversation turn until Señor Zinn was its center. Then I admitted—in a hushed way that suggested that only he also knew—that I was there to find out if Señor Zinn had drowned or died another way. After all, I said, the police had been far from the first ones on the scene. Didn't he himself come there early every morning—even at dawn?

I pulled out a huge banknote from my wallet and curled it into my hand so that we both knew how things would now proceed. He glanced along the seawall and down to the beach and, seeing that it was empty, made a flick of the eyes that gave the assent.

"Don't come any closer to me," he said. "Look away and talk in a normal voice."

I did exactly as I was told.

"Were you there that day?"

"I came down at six. The body was there, but there was someone else as well. It was a man I know. He fishes around here, but he has a house in the interior where he lives. I saw him turn the body over and go through the pockets. After that he left. He won't be back here for a long time."

"Why not?"

"I can't tell you why. You'll have to find him yourself."

I reached out, passed the note into his hand, and watched his face change complexion. He said the man lived in a small town called Nueva Italia on the road inland that went toward Pátzcuaro. Everyone called him Rubio Pez, but obviously it wasn't his real name. He had a house there, and when the fishing dried up he hid out sometimes for months at a time.

No one knew much about him. If I asked around I would find him, and when I did I could tell him Nestor sent me. If I paid Rubio well he might tell me what he had found and why he had gone into hiding. But I should be careful going after him. He wouldn't know who I was and he might overreact. It was a small town in the desert and there would be no one to help me.

"Is it really worth it?" he said at last.

"If he was the person who found Señor Zinn, it is."

"I am sure it was him."

I turned to the yacht, swan-like in the agate bay, and I asked him who it belonged to. He shrugged.

"Never seen that one before. They say it's an American group from Los Angeles. Film people maybe."

"Did they swim ashore yet?"

But he didn't answer—the Yankees didn't concern him. Their music didn't reach into his mind. I spent the better part of an hour with Nestor and still he said nothing more. There was no reason to talk if you'd already said what you wanted to say.

NUEVA ITALIA LAY some miles inland in a semidesert, its houses baked into submission. In the stillness of high noon my footfall was the only sound heard outside the town's Western Union pickup, the Caseta Telefónica Luna, where I asked about Rubio Pez and was told that he came in once a week to pick up money. I hadn't lost my touch. The woman even knew where he lived, in a shack north of town in a place called the Presa de Infiernillo. I went back out into the glare with a small hand-drawn map courtesy of a ten-dollar bill while swallows scattered around me, perfectly free in a free world, and behind their sound there was the great silence of a desert.

On either side of the northbound road, the land opened up into plains covered with saguaros, upon which sat an army of blackbirds. The map had marked the turnoff of a dirt road that swung at right angles to the main one, and I drove along it for five miles.

There were no shacks out there except his, and it clung like a desperate barnacle to the top of a bluff infested with the same birds. Perhaps they were waiting for the lone occupant to die. I parked the car a hundred yards from his door and took out my *shikomizue* sword-cane from the back seat. The wind kicked up a blinding dust as I struggled uphill to the shack. It was made of a mixture of wood, aluminum, and blue plastic. I called out his name and said in Spanish that Nestor had sent me. There was no answer, but the front door flapped open. Then I noticed something move far off out in the saguaros. Someone was standing among the giant cactus, watching me, and it was surely Rubio. I turned and went down a gully toward him, still calling his name.

At almost the same moment a shot rang out and the air above my right shoulder shuddered and caused my reflexes to recoil downward. But I kept cool and didn't overreact. A confrontation was the last thing I wanted. I called out again.

"I'll meet you at the house," I called out.

I turned back, exposing myself to a shot, and made my way to the shack. When I got there he was right behind me, a man older even than me, white stubbled, and with a look of wild fear in his eyes. He was armed with a shotgun and was not out there to kill rabbits. An ancient mariner lost on dry land and about to snap his cap. I could see at once that he was harmless. But men filled with fear are often the least harmless. I decided to go easy on him and come over all smiles and charm.

"You're a terrible shot," I said.

"No, I never miss."

So he had mistaken me for the one who would someday come to kill him.

"Shall we go inside?" I said.

He wasn't sure. He held the shotgun against his hip and looked me over. Finally he ushered me in through the door into his pathetic den, out of the dazzling sun.

It was filled with tackle, buoys, dried fish on lines, and knives. I told him who I was, and how much I would pay, even though it must have occurred to him that the easiest thing to do would be to shoot me, take it anyway, and bury me later in the arroyos.

But he was a gentle old-timer and not up for any real madness.

"Sit down," he said, lowered the gun, and laid it up.

I placed the money on the table between us and was frank. I wanted to know all about the man he had found on the beach in Caleta de Campos and what he had found on him. I told him I knew he had come here to hide and that none of it was his fault after all. I admitted I was from the insurance company and therefore on the right side of the law, as he would be if he told me everything.

"Whose law?" he asked.

It was a fair question.

"Well, the Americans, anyway," I said.

"It won't help here."

"The money will."

It was about a thousand dollars.

He eyed it, slowly relenting, and then I told him that no one would know it was from me. He was safe.

"You're a fisherman?"

He said he worked the coast at certain times of the year.

"You must see all the yachts that come and go. I heard they were mostly return visitors."

"They are."

"They're buying drugs, aren't they?"

He could sit on the sea wall and watch the small boats plying their trade between the beach and the yachts. The rich and the poor united by Acapulco Gold. That morning, however, he was preparing his boat to go hunting lobster. He was on the beach at 3 a.m., and there had been a small storm earlier in the evening. The sky was clear and the moon shone brightly.

"There was a big yacht in the bay and the lights were on."

"Was there a party on board?"

"Nothing of the sort. There didn't seem to be anyone there. After an hour I noticed the man washed up in the surf. I went down to see who it was."

"Señor Zinn?"

"Not at all. I went down to look at him and I saw it was a dead gringo filled with water, and I dragged him up onto the sand."

The man had been dead for an hour, he thought, although

73

he was no expert in things like that. He was in shorts and a short-sleeved shirt, and had a gold chain around his neck. A man in his sixties maybe, with thin limbs and close-cropped white hair and tattoos on his arms. Since the palapas were long closed, he was alone there with this body, and he admitted that he went through the pockets to see what he could find. He wasn't trying to steal. He just wanted to know who it was. He looked over to the yacht and made the obvious connection, but there was no one on deck, and although the lights were on there was no other sign of life. He found a waterproofed packet in the shirt's chest pocket with ID, a credit card, and some cash. They were all dry. He knew something was awry and that these items might be useful or valuable down the line. He asked me if he had been wrong to think that. I told him he had used his wits and used them quickly. But why, I said, had there been ID or a credit card there at all? He must have just carried it around with him all the time, as people do.

"Then you have it here," I said.

"The credit card, I didn't take. I didn't take the ID either. I knew it would be trouble. I left those. I took the cash—I admit that. I thought they wouldn't miss it. They couldn't prove it hadn't been lost in the sea."

"So you hid all the way up here because of the money you stole?"

"No, Señor."

For a moment the wind battering his walls was louder than the sound of his own breathing, and his eyes took leave of their sockets. No, he said again, he hadn't taken anything except the cash, but he had looked at the ID carefully and indeed it was Señor Zinn, but he was sure the man in that small photo was not the man on the beach. It was a different face, a different person entirely. He was so sure of it he decided to go to the police up on the road and tell them, which is what he did. But he waited awhile first. He said he sat on the beach and tried to think what he should do. Then, as he sat there in the dark, the yacht's lights went off and it began to move off toward open sea. In a few moments the yacht was gone. He got up and walked slowly up the road. Still he hesitated. No one but him had seen the body, but he was worried about the cash he had taken. It was possible that the soldiers at the roadblock would search him and find the two hundred dollars and then things would take an ugly turn. Nevertheless, he went. It was still dark when he approached four men at the roadblock and told them what he had found. They asked him to take them to the spot and he did. When they arrived there they made him wait by the palapas while they examined the body, turning it over with flashlights and talking among themselves. I asked him if he had mentioned to them the discrepancy between the ID and the real face, and he said he had not. He waited for them to notice it themselves.

But they did not.

They called out on their radios, and he thought about the money in his back pocket. They could easily search him and arrest him for theft and for tampering. But for a while they seemed to forget he was even there. At last, though, one of them came over to where he was sitting in the sand and asked him if Rubio knew who the dead gringo was or if he had taken anything from the body. With a straight face he answered that he didn't know the guy and that he hadn't taken anything from him.

"If we search and find dollars, we'll take you out, you understand that, right?"

Rubio held his ground.

I said, "You only took the dollars?"

He nodded, but then he added, "Well, there was something else. But nothing valuable."

He said that while he was going through the dead man's pockets he had found a slip of paper in one of the back pockets of the shorts. It had not been protected from the water and so it was sodden.

He got up and walked to his kitchen and pulled a book out of the cabinet there. It was a telephone book. Returning to the table, he opened it and I saw inside a small piece of paper, a receipt from an ATM machine. He had pressed and dried it and now it was almost legible. I picked it up and put on my glasses. It was dated from June of the previous year, in the town of Colima. It showed an amount drawn from the machine and the name of the cardholder who had withdrawn it: Paul A. Linder. The letters had almost faded away, but they were still decipherable.

I looked up to Rubio, and I saw at once that all the meager guile in his eyes had drained away.

"Paul A. Linder?" I said.

"That's what it says."

"You didn't show this to the soldiers?"

"No. I had a feeling that I shouldn't."

"So then what happened?"

"The soldier took me back to the road."

When they got there, he told Rubio to disappear and never come back. The soldier knew Rubio had taken the money from the dead man, but he didn't care—it was a way of getting rid of him. Rubio had walked down to the coconut grove behind the beach where he kept his motorbike and had driven south without waiting. It was still not yet dawn. He had not gone back since, and thought that his silence might be more important than he had once realized. So he kept his shotgun loaded and only went into Nueva Italia every couple of weeks to buy supplies. And now I had appeared and paid him a thousand dollars for a slip of paper from an ATM machine. He was on the brink of seeing the funny side of it.

"Mr. Linder," I said, "was the man dead on the beach at three in the morning?"

"He might be." Rubio shrugged. "He must be."

But there was no "must."

It was possible even that Rubio had misunderstood everything himself and that I had just paid him for nothing.

"Either way," I said, "you never saw that guy before at Caleta de Campos?"

"I never saw either of them."

"Zinn and Linder. Two German names. That's kind of amusing, isn't it?"

"If you say so."

I left the money on the table and blundered my way back through the door and into the blinding light and dust. He didn't follow me, or call out a farewell. I imagine he just sat there until all sound of me had receded, and then reached out to the roll of banknotes tied with a rubber band. His windfall had come after all, just as he had planned. I went back to the car and felt ashamed that I'd thought I'd need to use force against a sap like him. It was he who needed bullets, not me.

A mile from his shack I stopped and got out again. I wanted to see if he had come out to watch me leave, and so he had. I waved, and he turned back to the gloom of his shack. Back on the narrow road that wound its way north I stopped yet again and looked at the map. I realized I had no idea what to do now. Go back to the coast or press onward. It had to be the latter: whoever had abandoned his ID on a body in Caleta de Campos would never go back to the scene.

He would go in the opposite direction, inland, and maybe on this same road, though there were others. Had he passed this same lake surrounded by burned hills? By afternoon's end I was in Pátzcuaro, in a comfortable hotel on the town's main square, courtesy of Pacific Mutual. As dusk fell I went down to the lake and took a boat across to the island called Janitzio. I walked around it on the path that circles the whole island, passing under drying fishing nets and stopping to eat the fried fish of the lake they eat there. *Pescado blanco.* They look like little monsters. In this way I was thinking all the while, and yet I hadn't thought enough to find a way out of the forest of signs. It was sitting here, however, and watching the lights come on along the mainland, that I had the idea that Paul A. Linder was still, so to speak, alive and well. Zinn had now become Linder and was walking the earth with his former employee's name, a simple transfer that Zinn could use for a while until I caught up with him. He had slipped into his new identity so easily, and in a country where he was a foreigner anyway, that only I had noticed it. But he himself must have suddenly had the feeling that another man was walking over his grave.

NINE

T HE HOTEL FRONT DESK WAS ABLE TO SEND UP A GUIDE
to Mexico's luxury hotels, and over the next two days I
called all 207 of them in the top bracket. It was time consum-
ing and clumsy, but I had the time and I had the money,
and the town itself was a pleasant place to waste a few days.
At each hotel I asked if I could please speak to a Mr. Paul
Linder, and for the first 168 of them I was told that no such
person was staying with them. Something told me that it was
only a matter of time before a receptionist answered my request with a different reply. It was at the Hotel Morales in
Guadalajara. When I asked for Señor Linder the receptionist
said, without hesitating, "I think he checked out this morning. Let me verify for you." A minute later she returned to the
phone and asked who was calling.

"Señor Washington," I said.

The second absence was longer than the first, and this time
she said that Señor Linder was certainly not at the hotel now.

"Has he checked out?"

"Yes, Señor."

"What a nuisance. How can I get a hold of him?"

"Is it urgent?"

"In a way it is. I don't suppose you know where he has moved on to?"

She should have balked at a request like this, but it was a young girl, we were chatty and she forgot her hotel etiquette.

"Let me ask someone," she said.

I opened the map on the bed while waiting for her to find out where he had gone, and opened a red marker.

The receptionist returned to the line. "We think he drove to a place called Mazamitla."

"Is that a town nearby?"

"It's a village in the mountains. It's south of Lake Chapala."

"Wait a minute—let me find it."

With my glasses on, I did so. It was indeed a small village lost in the high hills with a single road leading to it. It was about a hundred miles from where I was sitting right then, and there were back roads that led to it from Pátzcuaro. An easy drive.

"Is there a hotel there?" I said.

"One or two. People go there for the waters."

"The waters?"

"There are swimming cenotes in the forests there. They're supposed to be healing."

"Are they?"

"Yes, Señor."

"Maybe he wasn't feeling well," I said.

There was a pause.

"He said he was feeling a little under the weather and I think our concierge recommended Mazamitla to him. It's a popular destination."

If he was driving down to Mazamitla from Guadalajara I calculated that it would take him almost as long as it would take me. It was then about ten in the morning. I went down to pay the bill and then returned to my room, where I spent half an hour dyeing my hair dark brown. It was the moment to adopt a disguise, to follow my prey more subtly and at a close distance. By now, accordingly, I had also grown a small trimmed mustache, which I colored with a lighter dye. The effect was disfiguring, but disguising. I looked like a grifter who likes the grift, a bum down on his luck. At midday I checked out of the hotel and drove north out of town toward a place called Zacapu, from where the westward route toward the great lake was fairly straightforward. When I was on it I relaxed a little and put Sinatra on the tape deck. My hands were sweating freely now and the predator in me had reawoken. Some of the juice of the glory days had come back with the music, and I remembered a thousand other road trips just like this one, voyages by moonlight during which I'd catch my eyes in the mirror and think, *not bad, you jelly bean.*

Clouds gathered overhead as I parked in the main square. There was not a soul in sight. Just a church with tiered towers infested with jungle birds. I saw a hotel nearby but decided to wait before going in and getting a room. It was likely that Zinn—now a harmless Señor Linder—was staying at the same hotel, though there was no rental car parked in the square other than mine. What had brought him here? Mazamitla was little more than a frontier outpost among the hills, indio to the core, a hamlet of old men like myself, of weary cats and a few dozen oil paintings of Father Hidalgo.

The hotel had an inner courtyard that had obviously once

been a stable, the rooms laced with dark beams, with rough-hewn log railings along the first floor. It was run by a group of women who were probably related. I asked them if the hotel was really as empty as it looked and they said, with some surprise, "*No, Señor, esta lleno.*" But there were two free rooms and I took one of them. I asked if they had seen any Americans wandering around the village, and they replied that they hadn't seen any at the hotel either. So it was possible that he wasn't there at all.

That would be inconvenient. I waited in my new room while the rain hammered on the roof and then went back down to the square when it had abated a little. The church itself was closed, so I walked instead out to the edge of the forests, where the ladies had told me the path down to the cenote lay. I took my Minox camera with me, ready to turn a lucky moment into physical proof.

On the downward path I passed gangs of woodcutters toiling away in the glades. They were silent as they swung their oiled axes in clouds of shavings and gnats. Their donkeys were tethered to the pines and at the bottom lay the sleepy pools and, as I'd been told, a waterfall. As I struggled along with my cane, one of the woodcutters came up to me, a child of about twelve, and asked me if I wanted to pay him to help me.

I had an idea. I gave him a dollar and asked him to go down to the cenote and see if anyone was swimming there. I sat against a tree and waited for him to return. When he did, he said that there was an old man alone in the pool swimming in his underwear. A gringo? Perhaps, the boy said. I said I would wait here for the man to come up on the path and let him go. There was only one path. But an hour passed and no one came up the path as I'd expected. The rain had stopped when I reluctantly gave up and went back to the village. I felt almost a fool. The same boy followed me up there, as if I were a possible source of more dollar notes, and he told me that people sometimes camped out down by the pools instead of staying at the hotels. I went into the church, now open and overflowing with white lilies and old ladies, and he followed me. But as we came into the nave, I saw that among the old ladies was a white man in a windbreaker sitting in the front pew with his back to us, apparently lost in his own thoughts.

"*Es el!*" the boy said, pointing, and slipped away again.

Instead of approaching him there, since a church is no place to make a scene, I went back outside and waited in the square. When the gringo exited from the church he was wearing a wide-brimmed straw hat and ambled across the square and into one of the streets that rose away from it. I followed him and soon the two of us were alone in the alleys, the cats scattering around us.

He was about my height but more stooped, inconspicuous in his windbreaker and baggy pants, and he seemed to know where he was going. I hung back, and eventually he turned into a doorway and entered a house.

I took a photograph both of his back and of the door, then went back to the hotel. I was still not sure whether it was Zinn. I could afford to tail him for a while until I was and had all the photographs I needed, at which point I could probably just fly back to San Diego and have done with it. I slept calmly at the hotel that night and got up early in order to eat my huevos rancheros in the courtyard with the ladies, who told me that the rain was going to continue all day.

From the hotel I could see everyone crossing the *zócalo*, the town square, and so it was a good vantage point, but by midmorning the old man of the night before had not reappeared. I went around the streets again looking for a car that might be his, but there was nothing. Then it occurred to me that there was also a local bus stop and there a few people were waiting in the rain for the next bus to arrive. Across from it a few men sat at a cantina; I asked them if they had seen an old gringo get on one of the buses that morning. Sure enough, they had. The previous bus that had left for Tuxpan two hours before.

I suddenly realized that he was trying to shake me, that he knew all about my call to the Hotel Morales and had taken off on a bus to make his trail go cold. Whoever he was, he might not know that I had followed him to Mazamitla, but he knew that someone was looking for Paul Linder.

I arrived in Tuxpan in the early afternoon. The weather had completely changed: a hot sun beat down on the Nevado de Colima volcano in the distance. The road passed by the silver mine, the hard hats walking home from their shifts along its edges. The corn milpas stood with a motionless attentiveness, glistening and juvenile, as if the plants had grown overnight. Here and there were men in tall hats, walking slowly down the lines of corn. A pale cloud clung to the tip of the Nevado, equally motionless and new. At Tuxpan's center stood a worn-down stone cross not unlike a Celtic cross in a village in Ireland, covered with what looked like runes. The cantinas were closed. A fair wind ruffled the dogs. In the town park there was a Volcano Eruption Warning board set up in the middle, with three color-coded alerts. That day the

Nevado was "mildly active." To one side, a line of abandoned train cars lay rusting on their tracks, a horizontal slum. Again, I was confused by a random stop in a random place. Zinn could as easily have hopped onto another bus from here.

I asked at the café by the cross. Yes, there was a bus that ran down to Colima and it had already left. The next one arrived in an hour.

Had he already taken it? I sat by the cross and watched the indios in the milpas slipping in and out of view and the miners plodding along the road. A man changing buses in places like this—it was a ruse and nothing else. The boys playing among the nettles were happy to let me know that an old white man had gotten off the bus from Mazamitla and carried on toward Colima. We gringos stick out and are easy to remember. I asked if he was carrying a bag. They said he was empty handed.

I went back to the car and found it surrounded by a crowd of small boys marveling at it. They scattered when they saw me, and I realized that there must be something terrible in my appearance, a ferocity I couldn't see myself when I looked into a mirror. All the same, I drove slowly down to Colima through slumbering villages, and it was late afternoon when I rolled into a city that looked as if it had been built at about the same time as Havana.

I felt slightly delirious by now. The town's cream-colored buildings struck me as airy whimsies built after many an earthquake. I parked by the gardens occupying the center of the *zócalo* and strode into the biggest hotel on the square, a place called the Cebolla. It was colonial and full of swagger and salutations. I liked it at once. A place of lanterns on chains and dozing habitués perched on sofas. I took a room on a hunch and then asked about Señor Linder. Yes, they confirmed, he was staying at the hotel. This was not brilliance on my part; there was only one decent hotel in the area. I even found out his room number on the floor above mine.

I then went back outside with a habanero and sat for a beer at the hotel terrace bar, where the mosquitoes were just getting started. My hands were shaking, and they hadn't shaken like that for some time, but by the time night fell a feeling of calm had returned. The air was filled with the whistling of pintails and soon a brass band started up in the park. I went for a walk in that park and saw that there were little signs on the grass that read *No pise al pasto*. For some reason they made me laugh. You can come to our town as an imposter, but don't tread on our grass.

TEN

HERE WERE TIMES WHEN I WOULD FIND MYSELF IN hotel rooms on the road in which I would wake surrounded by shabby wallpaper at four in the morning, surprised that I wasn't a boy anymore and why I wasn't waking up into my childhood bedroom with bees tapping at the windows and Mother operating a music box. Years of this kind of life wears you down and makes you porous. You die off bit by bit. The stale grit of the road gets into your unconscious, a small voice arises and says to you, "This is the last time, there won't be any more awakenings and thank God for that, eh?" A hotel room in Anaheim in 1957; another in Sacramento, maybe the late 1940s. The sound of jukeboxes and dive bars next door and characters long dead are suddenly alive again and chattering in my ear. Guys with names that people don't have anymore. A Malone, a Sam Something there, a Max over there by the window. A Lipschultz dead in his casino office. Even the old language has disappeared.

I slept through the morning in my cavernous room. Through my sleep moved old monsters and charlatans. The men beaten in alleyways decades ago, the women resigned to their twilights. A pedestrian alley of affluent shops ran along the side of the hotel where my window lay, and from it rose the musical sound of Nahuatl spoken by people sitting on the benches. I savored the ghosts while spinning slowly in the void of my dreams. In one of these dreams, a man I knew was walking along a tropical beach under a monsoon sky. He carried an ax over his shoulders and was whistling. I knew who he was. His name was Topsy Perlstein and he had been found dead inside a betting shop in Oxnard in 1953. I didn't know him at all, I just saw his face in the files and investigated his death. Why then does he come along our beach with an ax as if he knows how to use it, as if he knows me and I know him, whereas we are just together in my clattering dream? I can't say why Topsy has showed up in paradise, or why I showed up there either. I clutched at the cool fabric of my sheets, opened my eyes, then closed them again and thought, So maybe not the last time after all. There'll be one more time after this.

I reached out almost before I was awake again, and my hand didn't find the cane that I depended on. I turned on my side and a pain in my neck subsided a little. I looked across the room, and my first thought was that it was not the room I had taken the day before. It was a wealthy room all the same, colorless and elegant, its shutters opened an inch to let in the sunlight. On a secretaire stood a pile of old books, and the chair before it served as a prop for my cane, which had been placed against it. Yet now, there was nothing except the four-poster bed in which I was lying and a square carpet whose colors had faded to the point of indecipherability.

But then my vision blurred, I closed my eyes, and when I opened them a second time the room had changed again.

There was now a bottle of scotch on the table next to my bed. How had it gotten there and how had its ambrosia gotten under my tongue?

I dressed clumsily and went down to the hotel café on the street and got my usual *café de olla* with churros. The flies came down upon me, overjoyed and knowledgeable. There I was under the pale gray cathedral in the earthquake zone, and the streets were filled with children wearing party costumes of toy Aztec armor and holding toy atlatls as they gathered along the railings of the park. The heat beat down on my eyelids. It was the first day of the Easter *charreada*—the festival of the bulls—and among the children now loomed formidable women on horseback glittering with silver studs and chinelos with the faces of conquistadors. It was a spectacle for breakfast after a night of nightmares. The faces of the conquerors reimagined as cartoons, bright and mustachioed, with mascaraed eyes, whirling dervish–style, the Indian vision of European evil. It made me wonder again. Evil always has a face, a very human face that makes you question what goodness really is, or if it even exists. The faces of the chinelos brought back to life the faces of dead killers in my own past.

I had slipped the main waiter a handsome tip the night before and asked him to keep an eye out for Señor Linder who was staying on the third floor, and when he saw me he bent down to my ear and said, "Señor Linder went out this morning to Villa de Álvarez in the procession to the bullring there. That's what the bellboys told me." It was a walk of three miles, perhaps, and he would be gone all day.

I went back inside and found a concierge of wonderful corruptibility on duty in the main lobby, and during our conversation I told him—with some softening of the matter—what I wanted. I was an investigator and I would make it worth his while if he came with me to Senior Linder's room and let me in to have a look. If Linder came back unexpectedly we could claim it was an innocent confusion over the rooms.

He hesitated at first and then made sure that no one had overheard our entirely unethical chat. Then he pocketed the hundred and gave me a nod. We went up the grand staircases together, through the colonial halls echoing with trapped birds. On the third floor we found the landing empty and stepped quietly to Linder's door. He was clearly nervous, but a hundred dollars bought a lot in Colima. He turned the key, pushed the door in and let me step inside as if I was simply looking over a room for my own use. He gave me two minutes and no more.

To my surprise the room was exactly like mine and virtually empty. There was no luggage, no clothes, and in the bathroom there was only the hotel soap. Even the bed was made up as if no one had spent the night in it. There was not even a spare pair of shoes. I turned to the concierge.

"Are you sure there's someone staying here?"

"Yes, Señor. It is Señor Linder, as I said."

"But he has no luggage."

"That's his choice, is it not?"

"He's traveling like a ghost."

I went quickly around the bed looking for small clues, but there was nothing more remarkable than a half-burned cigarette in a glass ashtray on the night table. The curtains were drawn back, as were the shutters. I asked the man if Linder had left his passport with them. Naturally he had. We locked the door again and went downstairs to the office. Still behaving nervously, he went through the guests' passports until he found Linder's. It was a standard American passport and inside it was the profile of a "businessman" age seventy-two and born in Stockton, with seven years of validity left and a picture that did not look at first like the images of Zinn that I had with me but which slowly suggested a deeper similarity. The hair and mustache had been changed and the eyes were older, if anything, but I didn't need to look at it for very long before understanding that it wasn't the original Paul A. Linder. I looked at the edges of the photograph and I could see the forgery. It was a good job, but not that good a job. Enough to fool a hotel clerk or cross a land border without questions. I asked him if I could make a photocopy of the photo page and this required a further payment. Once I had it I asked him how long it would take to walk to Villa de Álvarez.

"For you," he said with a disdaining smile, "all day."

ELEVEN

A S I MADE MY WAY THROUGH THE CROWD, I LOOKED
for Linder under the jacarandas. The *charreada* festival
was in full swing and a procession made its way along a long
avenue, the snow of the Nevado levitating above it. It was a
movement as leisurely as that of a conga line at the end of a
party. In that high-altitude light the faces of the chinelos became even more nightmarish than they had been in the town
square, and I made my way through the mass as stealthily as
I could. But by the time the procession arrived at the wooden
bullring of La Petatera in the suburb of Villa de Álvarez, three
or four miles out of Colima, I still hadn't seen Linder. I was
waylaid anyway as I bought my ticket, and the guides rushing upon me sensed how soft and easy I was. They explained
in excitable sentences how La Petatera was built anew every
year for the festival, purely out of ropes, planks, and mats, or
petate. When all the bulls had been killed, it was all taken
down again like a tent, and the mats stored for the following
year. *Since 1943, Señor, and it has been built and dismantled
every year since!*

I climbed with the crowd up through the wooden plank
terraces until I came out into the open arena. There I settled
down with the Minox and my opera glasses, which I had

brought with me. The crowd by now was stamping its feet to the rhythms of mariachis, and the whole structure of ropes and mats shuddered under the assault. The ceremonial pandemonium had begun, and around the circumference of the arena a boy with a roller was painting the white circle anew. Opposite me the stalls were in full sunlight. I scanned them looking for my man and when I finally did see him he was in the sun, his eyes blinded despite the shades he was wearing, and I looked at him more closely through my opera glasses.

He was wearing an elegant summer suit this time, a buttonhole in his lapel, and a wide-brimmed Mexican hat. It was a startling change of dress for a man traveling with no luggage. He looked strangely small and slender from a distance. While I observed him, he himself watched the death throes of the bulls. As the day wore on, the area of shade moved leftward across the sand and eventually engulfed this elfin figure. Even if I had not been looking for him, I would have noticed him, because old men notice each other effortlessly. He applauded at each *estocada* death blow as the bulls slid to the ground with their tongues bursting out of their faces, and he did so like a connoisseur. Boys began wading through the crowd with paper cups of chopped soursops crying *"Guanábanas!"* and I ate mine while continuing to watch Linder eat his. Then, for a moment, gazing across the arena, I thought that he had spotted me in turn. I put down the glasses and turned away. The only two white men in La Petatera, one of them with a buttonhole, the other with a pair of opera glasses. At that moment a young matador was preparing his *estocada*. He had raised his sword and the arena fell into a hush. I was diverted by the moment, but when the sword had fallen and the animal had sunk to its knees, spewing blood, I looked up and found that Linder had disappeared. Uproar broke out as the kill was completed and I struggled to find the nearest exit.

Opposite La Petatera a fairground had opened for the evening and its lights had just come on. A fairground is always a maze, and he had disappeared into it purely to lose me. I was soon lost inside it, too, among the stalls of *nuez fina* and traveling shows—Tamara the Buried Girl, a girl sleeping under a plate of glass, the farmers gathered round to marvel at her suspended animation. This was where I saw him again, walking away from the same spectacle having left a peso note for Tamara.

I followed him. He moved like a sloth in linen, his legs long and still firm, his motions surprisingly smooth. The more I observed him, the more I became convinced that he was Zinn and that he knew who I was as well.

Behind us the Nevado glowed ashes-of-roses against the blue; its snow seemed more ominous and close than it had on the road. Linder appeared not to know where he was going but soon, guessing his way, beat a path back to the road. There were now mariachis in white suits roaming the byways, double basses held at those absurd angles. The spirits come alive and set to music. The pool halls by the road were in full swing, too. He crossed the road and seemed to flirt with the idea of playing a game there, but instead set off by himself along the road back to Colima, picking his way carefully as old men do and now apparently oblivious to my presence—if he had even been aware of it in the first place.

And so we went, one following the other along the same road that we had both come that afternoon, until Linder came to a cantina by the road and stopped there for a drink.

He laid his hat on one of the outdoor tables and ordered a shot of some kind and then lit up a cigar. For an hour he sat there puffing away and I sat on a wall in the shadows and watched him, taking note of the way he smoked, the way he lifted his glass, the way he drummed the tabletop with his fingers. He looked like a man who was comfortable in his surroundings, as if he had been there many times before. Then he was called inside by a waiter, got up, and vanished inside. Ten minutes later a car drew up outside the cantina and Linder reappeared, making a hasty move for its back door. They drove off. After a suitable pause I went to the same table. The waiter came out and wasn't extraordinarily welcoming. Linder's glass was still on the table along with a saucer of cracked pistachio shells. He offered to clear them away and I told him not to worry.

I sat, and while he got my order—a shot of *añejo*—I looked at the edge of the glass that Linder had just abandoned. There was a strange smear of what looked like lipstick around the rim. He hadn't finished the glass.

When the waiter returned I asked him if he knew every old gringo in Colima or just us two. "Not at all," he said, "that man is a stranger, too. Just as you are." He smiled at me and his eyes were knowing

"We Americans—we're everywhere!" I joked.

His smile was glacial.

"Not quite everywhere, Señor."

I paid for the drink and let it sit untouched on the table while he cleared away the nutshells. He stood there looking down at me as if suddenly realizing that he had made a mistake. He moved off then and did not return. I knocked back the *añejo* and waited for a taxi to pass on its way to Colima.

Back at the hotel I asked the concierge if Linder had returned. He confirmed that he had. Would the concierge do me a favor? Would he go up to the room and knock on the door and, when Linder answered, ask him if he needed a turndown for the evening?

I waited at the bar, where a few Americans were also drinking, and a few minutes later the concierge came in and told me that Señor Linder had answered the door and that he had been dressed in a silk robe.

"A silk robe?"

"Yes, sir."

So Linder seemed to have a wardrobe now. I wondered if it had been delivered to his room.

"Is he alone in the room?"

"I am not aware of a woman, if that is what you are asking."

I showed him the photo I now always kept of Zinn in my pocket.

"Was it this man?"

"I think it is," he said.

"*Bueno,*" I thought. Bird in the hand.

I might have felt exultant in the old days, but now I felt nothing but a quiet relief. An hour later I went up myself to the third floor and sat on the bench that stood on the main landing, surrounded by old Spanish *baúls*. The birds still swooped down the galleries, lamenting their baffling imprisonment. Though I wanted to, I resisted the urge to knock on his door myself. The opportunity to gather more evidence while still unknown to him won out, and I decided to wait and go back to my room. Before I did, however, I stood in the corridor and listened. There was the faint sound of a radio and nothing more.

In my room I lay on the bed and tried to think it through. Pacific Mutual had not asked me to bring him in, and I didn't have any jurisdiction to do so. All they wanted was evidence, and this was not even what they had been looking for. It was not what I had been looking for. It occurred to me that if I wanted to I could easily make a deal with him. I could scare him a little and then agree to leave him alone for a small cut of the take. It wasn't very noble, and it was against my best instincts, but there wasn't anything particularly noble about anyone else either. Pacific Mutual's profits meant nothing to me, and Zinn's scam didn't concern me either.

Many a man has staged his own death to dupe an insurance company. The companies in the States had no advanced database with which to cross-check claims; it was all done laboriously by hand as in the days of Dickens. Most companies would cautiously refuse a payment, but one or two would pay out and that would be enough to milk a million and then disappear. It was no doubt what Zinn had done.

But there was the matter of the real Linder. Maybe I owed something to him, the poor heel, tossed against his will onto a beach for the sake of someone else's scheme. One always owes something to the silent ones who are victims of other people's circumstances. It was to him I felt an allegiance now. Maybe he had a wife or a sister I could return to with a version of the truth. It was not nothing.

I must have fallen asleep then, because it was almost midnight when someone knocked on my door. It woke me up and for a moment, just as on that same morning, I had no idea where I was. It was a stealthy, timid tap, but when I didn't answer it grew a little bolder. Through the peephole I saw the distended face of a woman, young and heavily made up, and there seemed to be a shadow or aura of someone else close to her but out of view. She knocked more loudly and I drew back from the door, waiting to spring, insofar as I can spring at my age. Finally they gave up and I heard shuffling on the carpet outside. There were certainly two of them, and I sat at the edge of the bed for a long time wondering about it. Perhaps they had gotten the wrong room, a pimp and his girl.

TWELVE

THAT NIGHT SLEEP DIDN'T COME. I TOOK OUT THE blade from my sword-cane and oiled it like some old samurai pondering his soul. I'd never used it on a person, but it was my last line of defense these days. When the muscles give out, there is always cold steel to defend you. That smith in Tokyo had made it years before out of the tamahagane "jewel steel" that is used to make *katana* swords. A blade made from iron sand, capable of cutting through other metals and made elegant by a genuine hamon tempering line. I couldn't live a day without it now.

In the morning I sat at the terrace outside in the heat with the coffee men in their cowboy shirts and waited for Linder to appear through the front doors. I wore my aviators and spread that morning's *Diario de Colima* wide enough to hide myself and drank my pots of *café de olla* with the usual churros. At nine fifteen Linder stepped out, pausing for a moment as the sun struck him in the face, and raised a hand to shield his eyes.

Blinded for a moment, he didn't see me. One of the bellboys behind him carried a small good-quality leather case with silver-colored buckles.

A rental car came down the street and stopped right in

front of them and they stepped with an improbable dignity toward it. My own car was parked in the hotel's lot at the rear of the building, and I asked the waiter to tell the staff to bring it around for me at once.

Linder, meanwhile, got into the driver's seat, and the boy who had accompanied him saluted, handed him the bag, and stepped back from the car.

He had been dressed like a normal businessman, the same pale suit he had worn to the bullfight, hair cropped close to the head. But his appearance had changed completely since the bullfight, as if he was growing into a new persona and doing so well.

My car arrived a minute after he had departed from the *zócalo*. On the outskirts of the city I picked him up again, heading for the fast road south to Manzanillo. So he was heading back to the coast.

He seemed like a man enjoying the first days of a tropical retirement. Fortune certainly was shining on him. And I had the feeling then that I had made a mistake about him up until now: he had no idea that he was being followed and he had no idea who or what I was. He was alone in his little world and that world was filled with sunlight and easy money. He had disappeared and reemerged and was sure that no one had noticed. It was the ease of those who know they can get away with things that other mortals can't. It's a type I know very well, perhaps better than any other. Unsurprisingly, he checked into Las Hadas. It's one of the most famous hotels in Mexico. Sprawling over an entire peninsula, it was like a film set of a film set representing a luxurious neighborhood in Tangier, which is to say: a thing that doesn't exist.

It was a magnet for stooges and men on the lam, bottom-feeders and little playboys with trim mustaches, Americans with yachts who could berth at its vast and private marina, and women looking for easy scores. Moorish white and filled with lagoon pools and villages-in-Andalucía streetlamps, with a scene that spilled over into restaurants and nightclubs filled with unknown famous people and well-known shadow men who stepped into the light for a brief moment with a mission to enjoy the moment.

I had been there before, but never on a job, and I had played golf on the immense course and watched the celebrity tennis tournaments with the stars of Mexican soaps I had never heard of, not to mention the stars of the local tennis club, Club Santiago. I sometimes saw Beau Bridges there, but most of the other stars were after my time and I had never kept up with them, though I recognized Ruta Lee and sometimes was tempted to ask her for an autograph. Cesar Romero on her arm, the sun upon their brows—those were the days, may they never return!

Linder and I arrived almost simultaneously, so I went straight into the lobby as if I were already a guest and waited until Linder had completed his formalities, then followed him and his bellboy up to the room he had been given. It was a suite with a view of the bay, and when I had ascertained the room number I went back down and checked in myself. I, too, asked for a suite with a view and, after they had suggested a few units far from Linder's, managed to narrow them down to a suite three doors down from his. Another hop took me to my room. The suite had marble pillars and a balcony with bougainvillea, and, seen from its balcony, the sea had a distantly nostalgic quality, a depth of blue I hadn't seen in years.

WHEN THE BELLHOP had gone, I put my hat back on and went to a corner of the large window and looked across to what I assumed was Linder's balcony. He was not there, but I saw a bathing suit laid across the back of one of the chairs. I then drew up a chair and sat by my door listening to the corridor.

Only a half hour later I heard a door click and someone pad down toward the stairwell. I opened the door quietly and saw Linder's form in swimming trunks and a golf shirt receding down the corridor. I followed him down to the lobby. From there he asked his way to one of the beachside restaurants and took a table there. It was almost happy hour and he asked for a menu. Turning back to the lobby, I found one of the service boys—I can read the corruptible ones by their faces—and asked him to help me back to my room. He was about eighteen, bored on the job, and on the way I asked him about his work. The pay was abominable, he said, but I suggested there were ways to make a little extra. When we were alone in the corridor, I asked if he'd slip me a duplicate key for Linder's room for a tip. I just needed it for thirty minutes. He hesitated, but the hesitation wasn't entirely serious and he quickly pocketed the hundred and set off back to the lobby to get the duplicate. It took two minutes. Not wanting to leave me alone, however, he came with me to Linder's door just as the concierge at the Cebello had. I stopped in my own room for a moment to pick up my listening device and then the boy let me into Linder's room.

It was just as orderly as the room had been at the other hotel, but now there was a suitcase laid on the floor and a pile of newspapers on the bedside table. I looked for a place to lay the bug and decided in the end to leave it under a corner of one of the rugs in the main room. It was so small no one would notice it, and the boy had told me that the maids only beat the rugs weekly. Leaving it there, we went out and the boy walked away without saying a word. I went down to the same restaurant and watched Linder eat his way through a plate of tacos.

Eventually, he got up and went down to the beach for a swim. While he was there I took pictures on the tiny Minox and recorded his pale, shriveled form emerging from the waves. He returned to the table and ordered a bottle of tequila.

There was always a commotion at Las Hadas at twilight. The guests came down to the beaches in their night finery, the live music started up, and the drunkenness began. It was time for Linder to go back to his room and dress up as well. I didn't follow him. I waited for fifteen minutes, then went to my room and opened up the radio transmitter for the bug. He was in the bathroom clattering about. There was a long period of silence and then the phone rang. He walked up to it, picked it up, and answered "Yes?"

There was nothing more before he put the phone down.

He went out onto the balcony and from the window I saw him sit at the table and take in the view. The whole bay was lit up by fishing boats. Then, at last, his doorbell rang and he went back into the room. A guest had arrived.

It was a man, and his voice rolled with a Mexican lilt when he spoke English.

"It's not bad," the guest said, evidently walking around the room and talking it in. "You got the best one."

"Want some rum?"

"Not yet. You coming down with me?"

"I'm dressed, aren't I?"

"You look like a dancer."

Linder had a voice like a child's, gentle and high. It came as a surprise. The words were sung as a kind of libretto.

"Where are we meeting Topper?" he sang.

"At the bar. He's already there getting friendly."

"Is that right? What a scoundrel."

"I told him you didn't want him to drink."

"Too late now."

They went to the door and opened it. I put on a jacket and followed them back down to the lobby. There was a party that night for the Thalians, an American society for children with mental health problems that was popular among Hollywood donors. The festivities were already under way and, as darkness fell, fireworks erupted into life on the beach and conga lines appeared in the surf. There was so much confusion that I failed to find Linder and his friends, not even in the bar where they were supposed to have met. At least, however, there were so many people of my age that I was more anonymous than usual. I went looking for them like a fisherman after shrimp.

At the pool I sat at the outdoor bar and watched the crowds surging around me until I was satisfied that my unsavory gentlemen had buried themselves elsewhere. I asked one of the waiters for a Cuban cigar from their menu and he brought me one, along with a gimlet made half-and-half with Rose's lime. But I thought about my wasted esophagus and laid it down on the bar in front of me and waited. The Thalians were going mad on the sand, and a man in Aztec garb was running up and down with firecrackers attached to his arms. I unwrapped the cigar and clipped it, then lit the end and waited for it to take. As I took in the first lungful— the best odor known to the race—I sensed someone about to sit down next to me.

First I saw the heliconia of his absurd shirt, then a tanned arm laid across the bar close to me, and a smell of something like sandalwood, only very faint, competed with the Cohiba Esplendido. How did I know that it was connected to my quarry, I wonder, even before I had half-turned and glanced up at his face—handsome, you might say, despite all the distressing events of a sixty-year life? He had eyes as blue as a husky's and his face had only just begun to succumb to gravity. He looked better than I did at that age, I had to admit, and the downward lines that scored his face were shallow and elastic. His skin had a limber, oiled quality that made it admirable from a distance of two feet. A man, I suddenly thought, who washes his face in ass's milk or some expensive Japanese serum.

He seemed not to have really noticed me, but then, I thought, no one sits next to someone else entirely by accident. There's always a reason, conscious or otherwise.

But be that as it may, he ordered an inferior Jack Daniel's for himself without glancing in my direction and took out a small toy top from his pocket and put it on the bar. He set it spinning with a flick of his fingers and watched it as it wobbled, stabilized, and then wobbled again.

"Funny, isn't it?" he said to the barman.

Then he finally turned to me.

"Care to give it a go, sir? They say it's good luck if you can keep it spinning for a minute."

"What if I can't?"

He smiled and there was a handshake in the gaze.

"It's bad luck. But you'll get over it."

The barman said, "I tried it last night and couldn't do it."

I reached out and took the metal top and spun it.

"That's the spirit," the man said. "You get better the more you do it."

The top hummed with a tiny noise and then collapsed at the forty-second mark.

"You didn't commit," he sighed.

"I never was any good with tops."

"I get it. But you're smoking a very nice cigar." He turned to the barman. "I want what he's smoking."

"Cohiba Esplendido."

"Yeah, one of those."

The husky eye turned on me.

"So, what are you in for, Mr. Gimlet?"

"Beating the wife," I said.

"Figures. It's a tough spot. Have you met the Thalians?"

The conga lines were shouting to the stars at this point.

"Not personally," I said.

"A charming group. You on your own?"

"Like I said—the wife had me put away."

He chuckled and the Cohiba arrived—but this time on a plate. It was quite a little ceremony. The barman clipped it for him.

"It's not much of a place for a man alone," he went on. "You must be the only man sat alone in the whole place. That's why I spotted you. A man alone, I thought, sitting at the bar with a cigar. The old gringo. There's always one."

"I'm always the oldest gringo at the bar. I like it that way."

"Do you? Don't you get a little lonely?"

He spun the top again while the barman lit the Cohiba for him and passed it to him. The toy spun continuously for over a minute and we inhaled the leaf of Cuba simultaneously.

"I always wonder why men travel alone," he continued. "Me, I have my business partners. They're somewhere around having a better time than me."

"Are they old as well?"

"Yeah, everyone's old now. It's a fine country for old men." I raised my glass for a tap—it was about time.

"Kampai," he said, and obliged.

"Maybe in the future everyone will be old and it will be better that way. We won't be so anxious about it."

"Yeah, but what about the *muchachas*?"

"Those days are behind me now," I said. "But there'll always be someone to make you happy."

"Maybe."

He rolled his cigar in his hand and his smile was quite elegant.

"You traveling down the coast?" he said.

"I'm retired up in Baja. I come down here for the surfing."

He laughed. "You're quite a funny guy."

I asked about himself.

"I'm here with my boss. He has a house near Barra de Navidad."

He spun the top yet again and we both watched it while the smoke from our mouths swirled around the glasses. I now had an uneasy feeling about him, from where I didn't know.

"If you feel like joining us for a drink," he went on, "please do. But I didn't catch your name."

"Waldstein."

"That's a cracker of a name. You don't look Jewish."

"I'm German."

"German genes. Can't beat those. We'll be at the Loco bar later if you want to join us. Feel free. Don't worry, we're fun."

"It's me who isn't fun."

As I got off my high stool and put out my Cohiba—the barman gave me a napkin to wrap it in so I could smoke the remainder later—he flicked his forefinger off his brow and gave me the charmer smile.

"I still say you look a little lonely, Waldstein. It's not a good thing to see."

But I went back to my room alone and sat in an armchair in the dark listening to my radio. The hours passed and the party outside reached me as an inhuman sound and the occasional flash of a pinwheel. Waldstein, I thought, where in hell had I obtained that name fished out from the unconscious with such ease? Then I remembered. He was one of the dead, too. A drunk who embezzled a betting company on Long

Island and who was killed with a screwdriver on a rainy night some year back when JFK was still breathing. One forgets everything except the name. And he wasn't a German, he was a Jew. His body was put into the trunk of a car outside a laundromat and was as small as a child's. I shouldn't have betrayed his memory. I shouldn't have betrayed my own memories, for that matter. Poor Waldstein: I told him I'd make it up to him. Then, an hour after midnight, the door of Linder's room opened and the man himself rolled into it, a little the worse for wear, stumbling against a table and cursing.

After crashing around the place he picked up the phone for the last time that night, and his voice was so low that it was hard to hear every word.

"We'll go up to Barra tomorrow—yeah, that's right—I don't care what he says—just pick up the suits and drive up there. Who's at the house? We want to be alone now. Got it?"

After the phone had been slammed down angrily he collapsed into his bed. Thereafter he made no sound. The snoring began. I turned off the radio and began to feel weak myself. My head was burning and throbbing after the drinks and heavy cigar and it was worse than usual, as if the man with the top had made it so with all his spinning and cheap talk. I went to bed and my legs barely took me there. I laid the cane next to me and felt an unusual paralysis making its way up my legs until it reached my hips. The room began to disintegrate as if in the first seconds of an earthquake, and the marble and plaster had begun to shift. I thought for a moment of calling reception, but when I had decided to do it my hand would not rise toward the phone; it disobeyed all commands and lay by my side as if wounded. Instead it was the phone that rang. I wanted to pick it up, but my hand continued in its state of mutiny as the rest of my body panicked in a quiet way that an observer would not have noticed. I felt my mind falling, like a man missing his step in the dark and tumbling over a cliff. And, of course, I was indeed that old man, and I had suddenly become the quarry.

THIRTEEN

THROUGH HOURS OF STARLESS DARKNESS I SLEPT WELL into the following afternoon. When I woke I saw that I had undressed at a single spot near the window and that I must have been out of my senses. I took a cold shower and sat on the balcony in the sun to warm up. As I sipped my room service coffee, I saw, on the neighboring balcony belonging to Linder, a late coffee service for two laid out on the table as if the occupants had also been up all night. Wasps hovered around the coffeepot, but there was a feeling of abandonment about his balcony—or there was until the glass doors opened and a woman stepped out into the sea glare and sun and sat with her back to me on the wall, a halved grapefruit in one hand and a small spoon in the other. Down the back of her rose silk blouse ran a vertical line of nacre buttons, and as she ate the grapefruit with the spoon, scooping out the segments, her back muscles didn't move. I was too surprised to move out of sight, and since it wasn't Linder I didn't mind much. But as I looked at the chignon and the back of her neck I knew almost at once that it was Dolores Araya.

I was too fascinated to move, and a thousand things passed through my mind in orchestrated disorder. I was about to get up and dart back into the room, but in that split second of deciding to do so she had half-turned her head, like an animal that senses a predator it cannot yet see. As she turned, she saw me immediately out of the corner of her eye and turned more fully. Despite my shoddy disguise she recognized me at a glance. I felt a jolt of longing and hopelessness. She was made up like a nightclub singer, and her lips, even in the afternoon, were fleshed out with rouge. She put down the spoon and the grapefruit, and her stare was harsh and incredulous. I could no longer move out of its way and had to brave the ferocity that emanated from her. Her lips moved and she said something, but there was no sound. She turned her whole body toward me and took off her sunglasses and I could see the dark-green edges of her pupils. Her face had drained of color and her hands gripped the edge of the balcony wall. We were too far away from each other for her to call over softly, and she didn't want to make a noise. Perhaps Linder was in the room. But the silent semaphore was enough.

She seemed to be calculating how many doors away I was, and when she had done so she went back through the glass doors. I also went back into my room, packed up the radio, hid it, and dressed in a Sulka tie and a cantaloupe shirt.

An hour passed before there was a knock on my door and I saw her through the spyhole standing in the corridor in the same rose blouse.

I remembered how sorry I had felt for her before, and then how un-sorry I had felt for her afterward. Now I smiled to myself and relished the way I had accidentally trapped her in honey, little fly that she was.

I opened the door wide and without pretending to be

amazed, I asked her to step inside—it wasn't the moment for phony theatrics and pretenses.

"I can't believe it" was all she said as she floated into the room and turned to confront me standing up, all Cleopatra in a rage, but more like Elizabeth Taylor as the Queen of the Nile. I closed the door and locked it behind me, and for the second time within a month we were alone.

"You," she said, stammering a little.

"I come in through keyholes like Peter Pan."

"Who's that?"

"Never mind." There was no play in her eyes at all. "Shall we go outside or stay here?"

"Are you joking?"

She glared at the still-open glass doors and I invited her instead to sit on the sofa. But I noticed something about her at once: there was an oval bruise on the side of her neck about the size of a thumb pad.

"You're not going to tell me—" she began.

"No, I'm not. I don't come here for vacations. I go to New Jersey for that."

"You little bastard," she sighed, looking me over as she sat and then glancing at the door.

"It's work," I said.

"It's slimy, whatever it is."

"I admit I'm a bit of a snail. By the way, what happened to your neck?"

For a moment her hand went up to the bruise and then she dropped it with a dismissive contempt for her own moment of weakness.

"I ran into a reindeer. What's it to you?"

"Lucky you ran into me instead, then."

"You're lucky I saw *you* first."

I asked her why.

"You'll find out," she sneered.

"You should be happy that I follow you around—it's a compliment."

She looked very precious in her white cotton pants and silk shirt, her pearl earrings and Patek watch. She had gone up in the world.

"Well, I'm lucky, then. What can I offer you?"

"I don't want a drink from you. I want to know what you're doing here."

I told her she knew what I was doing there. If she didn't, I could explain it.

"I should have known," she said.

"If you'd known, what would you have done?"

She said nothing, perched on the edge of the sofa with heron-like poise, her mind spinning behind the licorice lashes.

She would have done anything, I thought. Whatever was necessary.

"It's very cruel of you," she said then. "You don't know what we've been through."

"I know what the insurance has been through."

"You don't care about them. You're just getting paid. I'm talking about what he and I have been through."

I leaned back and had to admit I was enjoying it now. Her eyes had filled with the expected crocodilian tears, but they didn't go anywhere; they didn't fall, nor did they explode. I didn't believe them anyway.

"I don't know what you've been through," I said. "Maybe

Mr. Linder went through something as well. Is Donald enjoying his retirement?"

She looked stunned for a moment, but she was a master at crisis control.

"I would advise you not to talk to him," she said simply.

"I had no intention of talking to him. All I wanted was photographs, and I have those. I can take them back to San Diego and we're done."

"That's why I wanted to talk to you."

I said, watching her recompose her long limbs as her mind changed tack, "That's more like it. You're friendlier when you want to be."

"I don't want to be unfriendly, I just wasn't expecting to see you here. You probably think Donald knows all about you, but he doesn't. I didn't tell him. To be honest, I didn't think you would come here looking for him. I was wrong, I guess." Finally she relented a little and her tone warmed. "I want to know why you're doing this and what difference you think it makes now."

"That's a good question."

I'd thought about it already, but I hadn't come up with much of an answer. Transparently, it made no difference at all what I did now as far as the greater good was concerned. It only made a difference as to whether she and Donald would spend a few years behind bars. That was a small thing.

"What if I told you," she went on, "that it wasn't planned. That it all happened by accident. That a man died in an accident and Donald just decided to do it on the turn of a dime—he had the insane idea there on the spot. You wouldn't believe it, I suppose."

"I don't believe I would."

"What if I said that was the truth anyway? He's an opportunist. There's nothing more to it than that."

"That's like saying you believe in a flat earth. Do you?"

She brightened and her fingers relaxed.

"Maybe I do. It seems more logical to me—a flat earth. It's less frightening, don't you think?"

She was sweating, her face shiny and beautiful, childish in its eagerness.

"Even so," I said. "What you just said doesn't change much now."

"Maybe it doesn't legally, but I mean, morally—"

"That's a tricky word at the best of times. But now it's a word that shouldn't be on the air. Who was the sap?"

"He wasn't a sap. He was someone Donald knew."

"It's always good to have friends who remember you. Did Donald have a quiet affection for him? You're going to tell me now how he died."

She was suddenly flustered and lost her grip for a moment. Her lower lip moved uselessly for a moment before she took up the thread again:

"Maybe we should calm down a bit and think this over. There was nothing suspicious about Paul's death. Donald got a wild idea and ran with it. It was a terrible thing to do. But he did it. It's spilt milk now, isn't it? It doesn't make any difference to anyone. Pacific paid up—it's nothing to them. Don't tell me it's the principle of the thing. You don't believe that and I don't either."

But I said that it *was* the principle of the thing.

"I'd like to know who Linder was—I'm curious that way.

But if you don't want to tell me, I can find out some other way."

"Oh, please. You don't care about him. You're just here to blackmail us."

"Me?"

I had to laugh, and she didn't like it.

In fact, I pointed out, I hadn't expected to see her there at all. I'd never blackmailed anyone in my life.

"But you're blackmailing me now!" she burst out.

"I haven't asked for anything, Mrs. Zinn. I could, but I haven't. But now that you mention it, it's not a bad idea at all. The thing is, though, there's no reason to do it. I don't need the money, unless I wanted to give it to charity."

"I don't believe you," she shouted.

"Keep your voice down. Your fine husband might hear through the walls. By the way, how does he like being called Paul?"

"He doesn't care what he's called. He just wants to live his life."

Now the tears rolled.

She confessed to his massive debts. It was a way out—everyone wanted a way out. Didn't they?

"Not really," I said.

"Just because you've never been in a desperate situation. You don't even know what a desperate situation is. I'm not saying it wasn't our fault. But still, things get out of hand. It happens. It happens to ordinary people."

"Are you 'ordinary people'?"

"Of course we are. We just walked into an extraordinary

situation. We're not evil people, as I'm sure you think. I go to church."

"I doubt Donald does."

"He's a decent guy. He's probably more decent than you, come to think of it."

"That's a high level of indecency to match."

She got hold of herself a little and her eyes calmed down and dried. She seemed to realize that she had to be cunning now and not lose control of a delicate, rather than desperate, situation. Her eyes stilled and concentrated on the pathetic old man across the room from her. How could I not be managed as one manages a Pomeranian dog? It just required a little thought and discipline.

"We can be rational about this," she said quietly.

"Why don't you start from the beginning? There's no rush. We have all afternoon, unless your husband is waiting for you to go water-skiing?"

"No one's waiting for me."

I didn't ask her for her life story, nor even her history with Mr. Zinn. But she related it anyway.

As I had already heard, she met Donald while a waitress at the Flamingo Club in Mazatlán. Older men certainly don't have their charms, but they do have their uses and Donald had his. He was generous, careless with his cash, and given to expressions of wild emotion that struck women as genuine when they were in the moment but that seemed stranger when they woke up sober the next day. No matter. He had a way about him and she had liked him on the spot. So unusual, so extravagant. He used to come down to Mazatlán alone and marlin-fish with his friends. When things turned romantic he had invited her to California. It was every Mazatlán bar girl's dream. He took her on weekends to Julian in the mountains and to the 29 Palms Inn in the Mojave Desert; they went to fancy dinners at Mille Fleurs in Rancho Santa Fe and stayed at his townhouse in Coronado. When he asked her to marry him she had not hesitated for a moment. He was old but full of beans, as she put it, and he had property and money on an incomprehensible scale.

"You couldn't have blamed me," she said coyly, suddenly warming up again and seeming to relax. "And in the end, you and I are not so different, are we? You can say Donald is a con man, but he isn't a cheap one. I can't stand the cheap ones, can you? Of course you can't. Like me, you just want what you can get out of it."

"Are you going to make me an offer?"

"I'm still thinking. I'm wondering what kind of person you are. I couldn't do it without telling Donald, though. I can't give you a payday and make you go away behind his back."

I asked her if that was what she wanted, for me to just disappear.

"Sure," she said. It came with a beautiful smile.

"But Donald holds the purse strings. So I should meet him and he can see what he thinks?"

"I think that's best, don't you?"

"I'd say that was pretty dangerous for me," I said.

"You mean he might decide to kill you instead? Let's not be melodramatic. That would create all sorts of problems for us. We just want to be left alone, and I think you know that. We can have dinner, and after we pay you, we go our separate ways. It's easy money for you, I'd say. You can tell the insurance company whatever you want. They can't prove anything, and if you say so, they'll leave us alone."

"You worked it all out in five minutes."

I didn't really think this, of course. She had worked it out long before, and for that matter, the two of them had both worked it out. I could see what an effort she was making to keep her surface calm and composed. She was never going to flip her wig, but from time to time a little shudder broke the surface and there was nothing she could do to conceal it. In a way, it reassured me. There was human struggle there in her violent depths. She was not a machine or a complete fraud, and it was even possible that there existed, in those unseen depths, the last vestiges of a once functional conscience. Her smile was at first cold as she proceeded to the question of money, but it was not as cold as she wanted it to be: money was something she humanly understood and greed was something with which she instinctually sympathized.

"I don't think it's very complicated. But it depends of course how much you're asking. People usually ask for too much."

"I'm not asking anything," I said. "You can make your offer and I can decide whether it's worth taking."

"All right."

Her eyes narrowed and she was wondering what to accept or deny on the spot. Better to buy a little time.

"I'll have to discuss it with Donald—"

"You do whatever you want. Shall I meet you both downstairs at nine?"

"Let me ask him first. I mean, we have to discuss it. He might be very unpleasantly surprised."

"Let's assume the worst, shall we?"

"He's got a bad temper when he's surprised."

In younger days I would have tried a different tack and made a bid for her at that moment. Her vacillation and disgust would have drawn me in. But I am just the medaled veteran now, the man with slow legs and the gleaming metal chest. I am off the battlefield, as I had told the spinning-top man, and the moment came and went with nothing more than a thought or two. She got up, and I did as well, but with the usual struggle. She watched me with a slight disbelief. We went to the door. Her eye took in a few details of my room, the things that I might have hidden before her arrival, and then she turned before opening the door and told me that I would be better off taking their money and going home. Being retired wasn't so bad. It was better than a life like this. Living in hotel rooms in Mexico and spying on people.

"That's a miserable life for someone like you," she said.

"What would be a merry one?"

"Oh, I don't know. Sitting by the fire with your dog while your maid makes lasagna."

"That's what I'll go back to."

"It's a good plan. I think you should stick to it."

She pulled the door open herself and I thought she was afraid to go back to her room now.

"I'll let you know about dinner," she said, and slipped back out into the world in which she was so comfortable.

"I'll be waiting by the phone."

FOURTEEN

I N FACT I CALLED ROOM SERVICE AND ORDERED A GIM-
let and then called Bonhoeffer in El Centro. I knew exactly
where to find him. He was at the diner eating alone, as I supposed was his sorry wont, and the heat of the desert seeped
through the earpiece of the restaurant telephone. I was glad
not to be there.

"You do call," he said, "at the damnedest times." And yet
it was midafternoon. I said I wanted to know if he could trace
a Paul A. Linder for me for a modest fee. He wrote down the
details on a napkin and we came to an agreement about it: he
would call me back the next day.

"But off the top of your head?" I said.

"Never heard of him. He never crossed my path anyway."

"If he's from that county you'll find him. I'd check all the
vagrants, too. I don't know that he's respectable."

For a moment he stopped eating his vile burger.

"You're in Mexico? You sound happier already. Maybe
you shouldn't come back."

It was an idea, to say the least.

I set up the radio again and listened in to Zinn's room
a few doors down, where Dolores was pacing up and down
anxiously awaiting her mad prince. An hour went by until

he came. The door was garrulously thrown open, the sound of the lock being put in place, the whispers. They went out onto the balcony and I assumed that it was there that she explained to him what had happened. They came back inside and she was still explaining. His high singsong voice was full of threat and peril, but also with wonder and naïve amazement. For a while he went silent and she continued pacing the length of the room.

"Who is he?" he kept asking.

"He came to the resort. I didn't tell you because—"

"So now he's here."

"We'll pay him off. It's not a big deal."

Donald lay on the bed—the springs creaked—and she sat next to him. They whispered inaudibly for a while, the voices rising to little crescendos of panic once in a while, and then one of them ran a bath. At first I thought it was an old trick to drown out their talk, but it turned out it wasn't one they knew. He got in the bath and the room became still again. She spoke to him from the bed.

"We'll invite him up to the house for dinner and give him the money. Let's treat him calmly. He just wants a payoff."

"These bastards—"

She said, almost laughing, "It's just human nature. I can understand him. Let's invite him up to Barra and give him some good wine and a suitcase of money, and he'll leave happily. Then it's over."

"All these bastards are on the take. It makes me laugh."

She went to the bathroom and her voice receded. But I heard her say, "Leave it to me."

There was silence for a few minutes. Then I heard him get out of the bath and they lay on the bed together.

"He's got some nerve," I heard him say quietly. "He's got some fucking nerve."

"Yes, honey. He's got some nerve."

"But here we are. And he's right up our ass."

"Don't lose your cool, though. Let's have dinner with him and you can see what you think."

"All right."

"He's just some silly old man. He won't—"

"Yeah, well, that makes two of us."

They must have slept for the rest of the afternoon, because the transmission went quiet. Eventually I let it go and went to the balcony with the camera. The bay was now lit by a sun almost touching the horizon, and across its calm surface white sails were scattered like moths feeding on a pool of rainwater. The hotel beaches were, as always, gathering their energies for yet another evening of joy, and the lamps around the resort were beginning to come on, lighting up the turrets and palisades and little Andalusian archways.

I had looked at the map again and figured out that Barra was only a twenty-minute drive on the coast on the same road down which I had come a few days earlier. I had passed it without noticing it, only vaguely aware of the villas of the rich standing in jungle between the road and the sea. They could already have bought a home there in Linder's name, a perfect hideaway for their dark but affluent future. Who knew how much cash Dolores had brought with her from El Centro, the suitcases loaded into her car and undeclared at the border. Even I could not estimate it. It might have been millions, all placed on a single bet, because if she had been stopped by customs they might have lost it all in a few minutes. But then, I was sure she knew all the Mexican border agents and could have bought them off. She had the nerve to do it; and in the end she had more of that mystical quality than I did. She didn't think too much before acting, and that gave her a lightning speed when she did act. I was beginning to feel a grudging admiration for her. The evening deserved a Gucci tie, and I matched it with one of my old vests. I had a genius for looking like a man who had stepped out from another era with my clothes, but nothing else, intact. Thus armored, I waited for her call. At seven twenty it came.

"Meet us down at the beachside restaurant. There's a table under the name Mrs. Linder. We'll be outdoors and in a crowd. Someone will meet you in the lobby and pat you down."

"I hope he's handsome."

"Fifteen minutes from now?"

I went down early and, as she had said, a man was waiting for me in the chaos of the lobby, able to single me out effortlessly. A young Mexican in beach whites and espadrilles. He was friendly and took me into the gents', where he patted me down, wished me a good evening, and sent me on my way. Certified as harmless, I went out to the beach and claimed the table that had been reserved. There were four places set. I planted myself there and ordered another lime juice gimlet and then waited for the Zinns, or now the Linders, to show up. After half an hour I was beginning to think that I had been stood up, but as I called for the check for my drink,

Dolores appeared, made up for an evening at the nightclubs, but nevertheless alone.

She made her way to the table and apologized for being late, and then added that Donald was not feeling well and would not be joining us.

"You needn't ask if I'm making it up," she said as she sat. "It's the truth. He's old, you know. It gets like this. He might come down afterward."

"Maybe he's just upset."

"I didn't say he wasn't upset. He's *very* upset."

"Well, here I am anyway."

She suggested we eat some barracuda, and who could say no to that?

"No, thanks," I said. "I'm having the crab. And I'll stick to gimlets. You should try it, it's an old man's drink. It's as sweet as the stuff you give toddlers."

"I drink water these days."

"Barracuda and water. No wonder you're slim."

Strangely enough, it was a pleasant meal. We talked about California, as if for the moment there was no other business between us.

"You'll never go back," I said.

"I don't want to go back. I sold all the properties after Donald died."

"What about the people you owed money to?"

"Mexico's a wonderful country, don't you think? It's like a wood with so many trees no one can count or see between them. The investors—they're rich anyway. I'm not losing any sleep over them."

"Nor am I, to be honest."

"You're not a fool, I knew that. The only thing that matters in life is getting through it to the end without being broke."

"Then why is it such a tall order?"

"Money?" She suddenly reached over and picked up my gimlet to taste it. She grimaced and handed it back: it was an old man's drink, all right. The lime cordial was from another age.

She went on: "You have to have the right religion on your side."

When she was a child she used to pray with her sister at the shrines in Mazatlán to a cult called the Santa Muerte. The Holy Death was always represented as a skeleton Virgin Mary, also known as Our Lady of the Shadows. Goddess of luck and money, among other things. It was like the pagan cults they had in Naples in Italy, cults of drug dealers and criminals. In Mexico it was an underground faith. The shrines appeared spontaneously in the slum streets and people went to them as penitents, on their hands and knees before effigies of skeleton women in dark wigs and wrapped in white robes. The assassins thought that the Santa Muerte brought them prosperity.

"I'm not sure it doesn't," she said.

"Did you pray to her when you picked up Donald's ashes?"

She smiled without missing a beat and yet her eyes registered the moment all the same.

"That's all past now. And I don't see that it really concerns you at this point. I talked it over with Donald tonight and we agreed on a hundred thousand cash. I know it's way more than you're making on this case and it's practically free money from your point of view. We think it's a fair offer. You're not going to tell me now that it's unfair."

I pretended to think about it for a while, and it was gratifying to make her uneasy. Finally she got up and said she was going for a walk by the surf while I thought it over.

I watched her from the table, solitary and lost looking as she tramped through the waves among the party boys. She didn't quite fit the part that Donald had created for her. For one thing, she had her own mind and she made it up independently. I'd underestimated her before. She wasn't an Able Grable, and she wasn't a cheap muffin looking for easy money either. It was Donald who was the drip. Surely he was watching us now from some vantage point, his room balcony even. Hidden in the dark with a pair of binoculars, his husbandly pulse quickening a little.

But I had already changed my mind about her yet again. She no longer felt to me like the puppet master but the puppet. The violence came from elsewhere. It was not her circus. The bruise on her neck was not the sign of a master manipulator. When she came back to the table, half-soaked from the surf and happier, she seemed as fresh and real as anyone I could remember. I was slack happy for a bit and she seemed to notice the fact. She dropped her hair elastic onto the table and sat again, shimmering with little cold drops, and her skin was goose pimpled as she picked up a quencher and tipped it back. If she was sugar, I wanted to ask straight out if she was rationed. She would've confirmed it and shaken me off, but it was still almost worth trying. Instead, I said, "You seem like being among barracudas as well as eating them."

She paused before she said, "I think you're going to say yes."

"I am. But for a hundred twenty thousand. I know Donald will agree, so why don't we make a toast to it?"

She blinked, but that was all.

"All right," she drawled. "A hundred twenty thousand. I'm not going to bargain with you after all this."

"Shall we get a bottle of champagne?"

"What an insane idea." She threw up her hands and then shrugged. "All right."

I called the waiter over and made a bombastic demand for a bottle of Dom Pérignon.

"*Para servirle,*" he said, and gave Dolores a cool glance.

"He sees me here every night," she said when he had gone.

"You and the boys. Are the boys watching us now?"

"They probably are."

"You couldn't run away even if you wanted to."

When the champagne came I made a toast not to our deal but to her. I said I was sorry we'd met in such unpleasant circumstances and that she wouldn't see me again after I had been paid. We drank half the bottle and she didn't care if it went to her head. She said that I was to come up to their house in Barra de Navidad the following evening and collect the money there. They would make me dinner and it would be friendly because, despite all his faith in her, Donald wanted to take a look at me up close to be sure that I could be trusted. He wanted to see me himself.

I, too, wanted to meet Donald after all this chasing him through country towns. Having met him in the flesh, I supposed I could let him sink back into his obscurity while I sank back into mine—we'd be quits.

"I'd prefer it if you just gave me the cash now. But you won't, I guess. I can see you won't."

"No, he wants to ask you a few questions himself. I suppose you know that Las Hadas is crawling with Mexican police? We're not bringing money in here. Come to the house tomorrow and I'll make you sangria."

She paid the check and we finished the bottle, though in reality it was mostly me who finished it, then she got up and wished me a good night and told me that in the morning she would put directions to the house under my door. Eight o'clock for dinner? She had it all worked out.

I reached up and shook her hand and, seemingly satisfied, she walked off back toward the hotel, leaving me alone on the beach with two or three thoughts of my own, none of them valuable. I had the last glass of the Dom and drank it as slowly as I could while wondering what the instructions to be posted under my door would entail. When I got back to the room I switched on the bug, but they appeared not to be there. I didn't want to stay up listening to them anyway, and so I slept with a Valium and didn't dream. It was the first time I hadn't dreamt in years. What a fine life it would have been if the same had been true for all my nights.

In the morning, in any case, I went downstairs for my *café de olla* and read the American papers in one of the restaurants until I felt the need for an ocean swim. Later in the afternoon, Bonhoeffer called me from El Centro. To my surprise, and his, his errand had proved fruitful. He had found a Paul A. Linder, or rather found the traces of a man of that name, who had since disappeared without anyone knowing why. The man had a trailer home in Salton City, that settlement sitting on the edge of the inland sea of the same name a few miles north of El Centro and the border, and as far as Bonhoeffer could see he had no family waiting for him except an old father who also lived out in the desert and was hard to reach, as well as being half out of his mind. No one had missed Linder junior; he had worked as a part-time gardener and sold drugs down in Slab City, where the hippies lived.

"Tell me exactly what happened," I said.

FIFTEEN

ONHOEFFER HAD FOUND LINDER'S RECORDS IN Salton City and he had driven up there himself that morning to check them out. I knew that road so well, the mountains like great piles of ash mirrored in dead water. There's a place near there called Hellhole Palms. I always wondered what it would be like to retire there and have that on my card. The Torres Martinez Desert Cahuilla Indians live there, just below the other little hellhole called Mecca—and you have to admit the names of these places certainly have a sense of humor. I wondered if Salton City had an Avenida Salsipuedes, a street name I often saw in Mexico: Avenue Leave If You Can.

Bonhoeffer had found the address of a trailer park in a place called Glamis on the far side of the Salton Sea. It was a road called Horseshoe Lane, within walking distance of the Glamis North Hot Spring Resort, where Linder worked as a gardener.

With barely any sewage or electricity, Glamis was a frontier hamlet, dried to the bone, and it had been easy to find Linder's trailer.

"I knocked on the door, but there was no one there, of course. I found a neighbor and she told me Paul had gone away on a job. The place had a padlock on it, so he isn't there. I looked up his records—he was caught once selling heroin down in Niland. They let him off."

"Was he part of the commune in Slab City?"

This was a tiny alternative community lost in the desert, known for its dropouts and drug-induced outdoor sculptures.

"I went down there after. They all knew him, but he'd been gone a few months and they could no longer remember him. They're all stoned all the time. I couldn't find his old man. They say he drives around the desert by himself and has no fixed address. What do you want me to do?"

"Nothing. He'll show up somewhere."

"There's another funny thing."

"Oh?"

"I ran a search inside the Palm Dunes resort you mentioned. They were clearing it out before the new owners took possession and the workers found a marble urn in the basement. Definitely human ashes. Mrs. Zinn seems to have forgotten about it. I took it down to the station and we have it here. I don't suppose you'd like to enlighten me?"

"This is the problem with people today. They leave their loved ones in their basements and then forget about them."

"It does seem a bit degenerate."

"Maybe she was in a hurry? I can't enlighten you about who's in the urn. Maybe it's someone who owed her money."

He laughed and muttered, "More'n like."

"Keep the urn there and I'll pick it up from you later."

"You?"

"When I know who's in it. You won't mind knowing either."

"It's just an urn. It's not a crime scene."

"See if you could find the father at some point, would you? I'd like to know what he thinks."

I SPENT THE rest of the afternoon waiting in my room, listening to the bug, which relayed nothing more than the commotion of a maid tidying their affairs. It occurred to me that they had already left, but at about five o'clock the expected note was slipped under my door. It read: "Go down to the lobby at eight and follow the white Pontiac Grand Am to Barra. The driver will give you instructions to get to the house."

All right, I thought, I'll play along. It was a risk, but something egged me on and it wasn't just my curiosity—it was a need to look that sick bastard in the face and make him twist.

I was able to get into the suite with the duplicate key, and once there I went to find the bug and pulled it out from under the carpet. I then took a look around the room. The sheets had not yet been restored to order and there were toffee wrappers all over the floor around it. And yet hadn't the maid been there to tidy it? The bathroom, however, unlike the bedroom, was immaculate. They had swept out the suite with an admirable intensity of purpose, leaving not even a stray hair behind. Downstairs in the lobby, I asked the bellhop what time the Linders had checked out and he looked at his watch as if he had already forgotten the time.

"About an hour ago."

"Did you see them leave?"

"Yes, sir. They had their bags."

And now it seemed to me that I should do the same.

Packed and shaved, I arrived back down in the lobby with my bag at seven and after paying went to the Loco, ordered a gin and tonic, and sat there quietly waiting for my appointed time to come. I was glad to be exiting from that pleasure dome, and in the back of my mind the idea of returning home had already formed.

At five to eight I went out into the parking lot with my single bag made heavy by the listening device and hauled it to my car. But I had carefully packed my cash on my person, where it seemed the safest place for it to be. It was a clear night, and the wandering mariachis paid for by the hotel filled the air with the old music of better times. I found the white Grand Am, and there sitting in it was the same boy who had patted me down the night before.

His window was already rolled down.

"I'll have to pat you down again," he said. "But we'll do it on the road."

"Am I allowed to take my cane?"

"I wouldn't take your cane from you."

"I'd fall over without it. You wouldn't want that."

The idea was that I was to follow him in my car until we reached a spot where another pickup would meet us. We'd stay on Highway 200. It wasn't far.

"You didn't tell me your name," I said.

"We're all called José. Makes it easy for you."

The road south wound through a great forest, before turning onto a small winding track that led to a headland plunged in darkness and the somber glitter of the sea. It was a tiny cove called Cuastecomates.

A hotel stood there right on the water with a jetty next to

it and longtails hauled up on the beach with storm lamps around them. It was a rough two-story structure with a bar on the ground floor and a patio giving right onto the sand. José stopped behind the hotel and we got out and walked down to the patio. Inside the bar a jukebox was playing and two girls were dancing together, having decided that since there were no customers they might as well. The moon now hung right above the bay, and its pale papaya brilliance made the darkness around it feel constricting and oppressive. We sat outside and the girls brought out *micheladas* for us. Once they had gone back inside José patted me down as promised and we sat in our chairs and drank. Across the bay, two or three lights marked remote houses in the forest on the far side. That, he said, was where Señor Linder has his place. A boat would come and pick me up.

In the meantime he asked for a bowl of oranges. When they came he took one and began to peel it for me. He said they'd asked him to do it for me.

"I hate oranges." I said. "Eat it yourself."

"You hate oranges? No wonder you look so scrappy."

"There's a Punjabi saying. Oranges are the blood of wives."

"What?"

I laughed. But he also laughed along with me: so he wasn't a bad kid, all in all.

"That's a crazy saying," he sighed.

A few oranges later, a light appeared on the water and moved toward the hotel from the farther shore. We strolled down to the end of the jetty until the shape of a longtail could be seen moving against the bright reflections of the moon. As it approached, José wished me luck and told me that the same boat would take me back on the return. On the far side was a path that led up to the house; I couldn't miss it. He would not be there when I came back later. We shook hands and he walked off back to the hotel.

The man helming the longtail was a local. On the way over he told me that if I paid him now he would wait as long as I needed on the far side. There was no other work that night. I told him that would suit me fine. Though I was surprised my hosts had not made such an arrangement with him. No, he said, it was just the man who had dropped me off at the hotel and he had only paid one way. I had to wonder about that.

"But you'll wait for me?"

"Yes, sir. If you pay me now, I'll wait."

I gave him a few pesos and felt I could trust him.

We reached the headland and he cut the engine. I scrambled out onto the rocks as he tethered the boat. The waves battered it about, but he left the boat there and came with me onto dry land.

Pointing out the path, he said to just follow it up the side of the hill through the trees. The house was at the top. With my cane, I was able to climb to a point where I could look out over the sea. Below me, the longtail thrashed about on its tether and the man was now hidden from view. The headland was a place of singing trees and immense winds, and here and there, fragments of masonry stood in the undergrowth. I climbed up farther until I could see a wall, and a house behind it. It looked like a 1940s villa abandoned by owners who might have fallen on hard times, the walls Spanish in style, with tiled roofs, and the whitewash streaked with disrepair and nearly half a century of sea spray.

The gate was rusted away and the house was unlit. The gardens had overgrown and its trees, untrimmed for years, had reverted back to forest. Farther up, the path petered out and there were no other properties. I hesitated. Now I knew there'd be no Linder inside, but it's always the same—I am the cat who is curious. Then, from inside the house, I heard a faint music.

It was some old jazz, and it must have come from a radio. I went to the door and pulled a chain bell, which didn't ring. But the door was open anyway. I called out, pushing open the doors with my cane, and stepped into a vestibule whose roof had caved in, leaving a pile of debris on a checkered stone floor, and whose walls were covered with graffiti. A crashed bronze chandelier lay on its side within a mound of discolored glass droplets and curled dead leaves and its once impressive chain had broken up into segments.

From inside the maze of rooms, a candle's light appeared and I went toward it with the cane half-raised. The vestibule led directly into what had once been a hacienda-style salon in which, at a long dinner table covered with bricks and small piles of shells, a man sat with a candlestick eating salami from a piece of waxed paper. He looked up as I shambled in and his look was cool and unsurprised. It was the man from the bar the other night, the man with the spinning top. So it had been a mistake to come.

"Am I late?"

It must have been my tone that amused him, and the

husky eyes were now not entirely hostile. There was a time, no doubt, when I would have been afraid, but at that moment I felt no fear whatsoever. When a man can already see his end the means of passing through it don't matter that much. His joviality remained undimmed.

"No, you're right on time. Salami?"

"No, I'm fine."

"Then we're all good."

There was a hunk of dry bread next to the waxed paper and on it lay a long carving knife. He leaned back and looked almost relieved. He was now in a leather jacket and a white scarf.

"The oven's not working, so I couldn't make you a pheasant roast. I'm afraid I'm a terrible host. Not only that—the Linders are away fishing."

"I gathered."

"Are you happy to be here?"

"I was expecting fire-eaters."

"Oh, them. They're indisposed as well. It's just you, me, and the salami. We'll have to make do by ourselves. Please, take a seat. I can offer you some stale bread, though. It goes well with the salami."

Ill met by candlelight, then. I felt calm enough as I sat down opposite him. It wasn't such a bad place to die, come to think of it. He'd bury me in the garden under the apricot tree. My decomposition would make it bloom.

"You're looking robust after that climb. Did you wonder if you'd have to go down again? Or whether the old man will wait for you with the boat? He only comes when I turn on the flashlight here."

He reached down and put it on the table.

"So to get out of this place you need to have the flashlight. See how fun it can be?"

I saw his point and said so. And now my ears began to work, anxious about sounds behind me in the dark, feet moving toward me across the floors of an abandoned house.

"You remember this?"

He took out his top and put it on the table and set it spinning.

"It calms me down," he went on. "You have to admit, life is very stressful. I find *you* very stressful."

"Me, I'm a breeze."

"But they don't like you. That's the problem we have here. You're not as popular as you think you are. Personally, I rather like you. You're a nice old gentleman. But there we are. Likes and dislikes are for little boys."

"I realized that a long time ago. It's a shame—I was looking forward to Mrs. Linder making me deviled eggs and a martini."

"You'll never know. But it's you who got greedy and over-eager. It's a bad thing to be in this world. I thought you'd know that by now."

"It's always curiosity that kills cats. But that's why they have lives in the plural and some to spare. I never could get over my curiosity. It's really a bitch, as they say."

"And look where it led you."

I looked up at the still-plastered walls, the windows with their metal shutters, and the faint shadows where pictures once hung.

"I had a feeling I'd end up here," I said. There was more

doom in my head than I was prepared to let on. "In fact, I had a definite feeling. I've had it for years. Isn't that strange?"

"Not at all. I have those dreams, too. We all know where we're going to meet the end of our road. It's a funny thing."

He stopped the top and pocketed it. The wind suddenly slammed against the walls and the whole house creaked. The husky eyes had slowed and finally come to a stop, and in return I smiled.

"Well, I guess I should be on my way now."

"You're a real old-timer. I like you. It's a shame, in my opinion—but anyway there's the door if you want to go for it."

He got up and picked up the carving knife, and there was a sad slowness resembling a reluctance in his motion. I got up as well, but with more confusion, and struggled to hold the cane firmly. He had not even taken my crutch into consideration and his eye did not track it. He stepped around the table and I fell back toward the door through which I'd come.

It was a ballet for which all my muscles were trained by decades of burlesque violence—by a thousand violent Carnivals and their tawdry dances. Unsheathed suddenly, my blade swung around as he came in and, as his knife sliced into my left arm, it fell into his shoulder, ripping open the leather of his jacket. He was astonished at his mistake, and by the sudden appearance of the blade, and wasn't quick enough to pull back his own and lash out again. Instead he spun around and stared at the cut in the fabric and his blood that had come rushing out of it. I had time, then, to swing again and this time caught him clumsily on the right leg with the flat of the blade. He came to his senses and his eyes lost their initial wild surprise. He was more like a dog than even I had realized when I first saw him at the bar, and his limbs had the stocky malice of hounds when their ire is up. His knife had been sharpened on a whetstone and it had cut beautifully: blood was running down my arm and onto my foot. I stumbled to the door and from there it was a straight line back to the outside world. But he was cursing at his own mistake and at me, and in the din I couldn't think. I was almost counting the drops falling from my arm onto the filthy checkered stone underfoot. Out toward the apricot trees and the broken wall filled with bird nests, I thought I could outrun him since he was more wounded than I was, but then I thought of the path falling like a precipice back down to the sea and knew it wouldn't work. He would catch up because I hadn't managed to cut up his leg. I turned in the vestibule, in dust and cobwebs, and slashed the leg that came at me. This time the edge cut into his shin and he howled and dropped to his knees. I staggered out into the path.

He had rolled over as if in resignation and lay there breathing heavily, and just as I began to move off I remembered that I had forgotten the flashlight. It was too bad, but I didn't want to step over his semiconscious body to get it. I had to rest for a while, wipe down the blade, slot it back into the cane, and then catch my breath.

The cut was deeper than I had thought and I had to calculate how much time I had before I would pass out.

I got back down to the rocks, leaving a trail of blood behind me, and made a tourniquet out of my own shirtsleeve. The longtail was still tethered to the rocks there, as if the fisherman had hedged his bets after all. He soon emerged from under the trees and in his face there was neither surprise nor horror. He must have known all along, in the calm way of all middlemen and fixers who have no stake in the game. He didn't say a word, just helped me onto the boat and cast off into the moonlit bay. We crossed in a few minutes. By now it was surprisingly late, as if hours had passed, and the hotel was silent. I gave him a bloodied wad of dollars and he helped me up to one of the hammocks still slung on the terrace. He asked me what I was going to do.

"My car is behind the hotel."

"You can't drive like that. I'll call someone."

"Just take me to the car."

He ran off to find it, but when he came back said it had gone. There were no cars there at all.

They removed all the traces, I thought. Good boys.

"Call a taxi," I said.

"For where?"

"To Las Hadas."

Because I couldn't think of anything else.

"Are you serious?" he hissed.

"All right, Paris will do."

I was in the hammock now and fading fast. The blood was forming a pool underneath me and the amateur tourniquet could no longer staunch it. He said I would bleed to death if I didn't get to a hospital. Flustered, he began to think harder. But it was too late; darkness bloomed in front of my eyes and I passed out before an idea had occurred to him. I spun on the surface of a great pool of oil and yet I didn't sink.

In my hammock I floated through the years. Artie Shaw came out of the stillness, someone singing about a choo-choo train and the lyrics I knew from the beautiful years:

Mama done tol' me, when I was in knee pants, a woman'll sweet-talk, and give ya the big eye. And I was singing along, rowing with my hands under the volcano. *But when the sweet talkin's done, a woman's a two-face, a worrisome thing.* I tried to remember where I knew it from, but then back in the day it was everywhere on the radio, night and day during the war, in the very first days when we were still happy. But I was in my twenties then and full of disbelief about nobility and charm. I already knew about the worrisome things. I knew that even Los Angeles at the end of its long golden summer was a place doomed to turn into what it eventually became. Paris, though. Paris in the rain. What I would have done for a leisurely stroll down the Boulevard Haussmann.

SIXTEEN

NSTEAD I WOKE TO FIND MYSELF IN A ROOM WITH high rafters and the small heat-repelling windows of the Spanish. Yet they were open and the insects shrilled outside, and I knew from that alone that I wasn't dead. Music drifted in from somewhere out in the night: waltzes, tango, or some such, the swaying hips of Buenos Aires and men in slicked hair cutting a rug. It was a tune by Antonio Lauro. On the walls, saints and monks and Castilian patriarchs in ruffs, tongs, and crucifixes and little ceremonial daggers. I was in a four-poster with brocade sashes. There was a mosquito net spooled on a ring above me and my arm was heavily bandaged and locked into position in a sling. On a chair my clothes were neatly folded and I could tell at once that they had been washed and ironed. So days had passed.

By the bed was a little brass service bell, so I rang it to see what would happen. Nothing happened. Under the door there was light, but no one came at the beck and call of the bell.

Could I move, was I paralyzed? Is the mind still here where the body is? But I found I could sit up and swing my legs out of the bed without difficulty. Below me, as if waiting for this very event, lay a pair of velvet maroon slippers. And now I noticed that I was in someone else's pajamas. They were striped like toothpaste and made of heavy flannel. I eased myself into the slippers and stood up. There was no pain in my arm, because there was no feeling in it at all. Someone had seen to that. I shuffled across the room to the window and looked out. A garden with fruit trees was surrounded by a wall with tiles and barbed wire lines. There was the faint glow of a swimming pool.

The air was still saline, so I knew that I had not traveled far. The sea was still there, if only out of view. The coolness revealed it.

On the back of the door hung a luxurious dressing gown that looked like a relic from the '20s. I put it on with difficulty. The corridor, when I peered out, was like something in a high-class liner. The boards had a dark-rose tint and were polished to the shine of Macassar on auburn hair. I crept down it to a stairwell and saw the light of a salon projected upward onto the moribund faces of yet more ruffed Castilians. The tango was coming from a vinyl with scratches. I lowered myself down the stairwell until I was in view of the room itself—an opulent colonial hall with beams and black viceregal furniture.

There was a long table here, but it wasn't set. The French windows were open to the garden instead, where candlelight flickered through the glass doors. The masters, whoever they were, were having dinner there.

I made my way across the Afghan carpets until I was almost at the doors, and there a young maid in uniform came through them holding an empty decanter. She saw me at once but didn't start; they were probably expecting me. She merely glanced at the table behind her and nodded to it for my benefit, then whisked herself around me. When I turned to see her go, I noticed that she was barefoot. I went to the door and saw the table. At one end, an old man sat with his back to me, eating alone.

But he sensed me at once and half turned in his baronial chair.

He was in his high eighties, I would have said, with the speckled head of a thrush egg, in his best duds for the soi-rée in his own living room. He wore a black-velvet smoking jacket and matching Albert slippers with embroidered gold crowns. On the table in front of him were Talavera plates piled with enough food for ten people, including a roast hen and pieces of a suckling pig, and a glass half-filled with red wine. A second place was set, though there was no sign of a second guest other than myself.

When I came to his side, however, he fumbled for a pair of eyeglasses lying at his side, put them onto his nose, and then glared at me.

"Who the hell are you?" he said in Spanish.

"I'm in the room upstairs."

"Are you now? Well, you should sit down and eat. Why are you walking around in a dressing gown?"

I pulled out the chair in front of the place that had been set and sat down.

"I was asleep, and when I woke up I felt like putting it on."

"Is that so? And how did you get upstairs?"

"I have no idea at all."

It seemed to be coming back to him now.

"Ah, now I remember. You're the gringo from Cuasteco-mates."

"I guess I must be."

"A man brought you in. I'm Dr. Quiñones."

I extended my hand: "Barry Waldstein. I'm very grateful to you."

Ignoring the hand, he suggested I eat something.

"I was expecting someone, but I've forgotten who it was. Maybe it was you. But then again, maybe not. My memory's shot to pieces."

"Maybe it was me, then."

"By God I think it was."

How long had it been? I kept thinking.

"I must have been in a bad way when I came in."

"You were sliced up with a carving knife."

He chuckled and turned abruptly to the French windows.

"Ana! Are you bringing out that decanter?"

"Someone put me back together again," I said. "Humpty Dumpty that I was."

"It was me, Waldstein. You may as well know you had a fair amount of dollars on your person and this was deducted. You won't mind, I know."

"I'd say it was fair all round. May I ask how much you took?"

"A couple hundred."

Well, it's a good private clinic, I thought.

There was a long knife lying next to the roasted hen and I reached out for it.

"No, no," he cried. "The maid does all that. You'd only ruin it. With one arm and all—"

She was soon back, decanter armed, knife ready. She carved up the hen and I felt myself slowly coming back to life.

"That's a very pretty bandage," he said. "Normally I'm retired, but the circumstances were unusual. I had to obey the oath. You have a five-inch cut that went almost to the bone. I considered getting you a blood transfusion."

The maid poured me a glass of wine and the doctor and I touched glasses. The old goat in him was all too alive. It glittered with mischief and puns and the rebellion against boredom that makes the old so anarchic.

It was me who was boringly earnest.

"Was it the driver who brought me here?"

"Not a driver. A friend of mine. A young doctor who lives nearby. He took a cut, too, for his trouble."

"I see, so he brought me here himself."

"He wasn't going to throw you back in the street."

"But when was this?"

"Today's Wednesday. Two days ago. If you're in pain I can give you another injection."

"I'm not writhing yet."

"So I see. You won't be able to use your arm for a little while. The sling will have to stay on too."

"I'll miss playing Rachmaninoff on the piano. But otherwise I'll manage."

"Let's drink to your left arm."

We did so, and the doctor watched me eat one-handed. He was not curious; he was not incurious. He was notational.

"It's a wild story. Mr. Waldstein. A man is found unconscious in a popular hotel that only Mexicans go to. There's no reason you should be there. And you're cut up like a side of beef. There's no weapon and no other person has been found. But we know you come from the other side in a boat."

"Do the police know?"

"No one told them. But who was on the other side of the bay? You don't have to tell. But, then again, it's just between you and me."

I said, reluctantly, "A business associate with a grudge."

"Oh, so that's it. It's always that."

"Nine times out of ten. They're the ones who want to take a bite out of you."

"Mexican?"

"American."

But the eyes didn't believe me and so I cooked up a feeble story. He took it in as if it was his duty to be polite.

"God knows why you people come down here," he said eventually. "What are you looking for? There's nothing you can't find in your own country."

"Except the chance to disappear. You can't disappear in the States."

"Well, there's that. But you're not trying to disappear."

"I might if I could."

It was then that I stopped and looked up at the sky. The Pleiades visible to the naked eye. Where were we?

"A few miles inland," was all he said in answer to this. "There's nothing to worry about. I'm a respectable man around here. As you can see—"

"It's a fine house. Are you married?"

"No, sir. Only the maid. She doesn't have much of a life here, but she can save up and abandon me whenever she wants."

"Well, either way I owe you an immense favor. It wasn't something you had to do, oath or no oath."

"Nothing to thank me for. I thought you'd been mugged on the road. But then again, why were you on the road anyway? And how did you get to Cuastecomates?"

"I drove there from Las Hadas. It wasn't hard."

"Would you like to be taken back to the Las Hadas?"

"I don't think that's a good idea, if you don't mind. I checked out and I had everything with me."

"Which is to say, nothing at all. You don't even have a passport on you. Just a lot of money and a cane. They're both in my safe."

"I must've been robbed, as you can see. I don't remember anything about it, to tell you the truth."

"Isn't amnesia wonderful?"

He laughed, but his eyes didn't lose their mark for a moment.

"I couldn't live without it," I said.

"You can say that again, young man. Amnesia is the only thing worth looking forward to."

I had no idea what time it was, or what the date was. Everything had slipped away between my fingers. The Pleiades were fixed and the tree frogs around the swimming pool wrapped us in their song. The candle flames flickered for a second and then restabilized. The doctor crossed his legs, the two gold crowns of his Albert slippers stacked on top of each other. Maybe later that night I wouldn't remember any of this either. It was all a dream and I had walked into it in slippers.

I ate for a while and then noticed that the doctor had fallen silent. Looking up, I saw that he had nodded off.

The maid crept up to the table and nudged him, but he didn't awake. We exchanged a merry look and she reached out to his glass, lifted it off the table. and took a sip. A moment later Quiñones came to.

"May I ask," he said, as if his stream of thought had merely been broken by a nap and had suddenly come back to him, "what you intend to do now? You can stay for a few extra days if you like. But I imagine you will want to go home. We can call your family, but we had no idea who they are. Do you?"

"It's a good question."

"Or are you all alone, traveling through Mexico? You said you had business dealings—"

I thought the time had come for a bit of honesty. The doctor might be able to help, and I couldn't pretend I was on holiday.

I said, "I'm looking for someone."

At this his curiosity and liveliness returned.

"Naturally. A fellow American—a man who ran away from his debts. I read detective novels, too, as you see."

"He's a man who has been around here for the last few months. Maybe you ran into him?"

But the name Paul Linder had not touched his ears. I filled him in. The husband-and-wife team, the jilt, the near-miss at Las Hadas, the real estate deals not only along the coast but also as it happened around the Salton Sea. I came clean about myself as well. I had nothing to lose and I was sure he would sympathize.

And so he did.

"You should have said earlier. There's something I should tell you. The boatman took two men from the hotel across the bay and up the path to the top. They found a lot of blood in the abandoned house there. I can't say if they told the police about it, but nobody from the *delegación* showed up."

So they kept their mouths shut, I thought.

But there was something else. The same boatman had gone back because a signal from the flashlight had summoned him. He had returned and picked up the other man and brought him over to the mainland as well, but an hour later—a comedy of sorts. By then, of course, I was long gone. The boatman had helped the man to his car although he had difficulty walking. It had been another American, also badly cut. The boatman had put him in the driving seat and asked him if he could drive. He had almost passed out. The boatman, however, took down the plate number in case the police asked him. The doctor had sent his secretary down to Cuastecomates to bribe him the following day and had obtained the plate number and a description of the wounded man as well as the car itself, the white Pontiac Grand Am. Quiñones had wanted to wait to talk to me before he did anything. But a plate number could be traced if he asked his friends in the Mexican police to help him. It wouldn't take more than a day or two for something to come in. Since no one had pressed any charges and no witnesses had come forward, and since there was no evidence of any wrongdoing in these dealings between two unknown gringos, there was no urgency on the police side. He could arrange to make it a private inquiry if I liked. I did like. All I wanted to know was where Topper had gone in his vulgar chariot. I didn't know who he was or what his real name was.

An hour later, as we were playing chess, Quiñones nodded off again. This time I got up and made my way back into the house. When he woke again he probably wouldn't remember that I'd ever been there, but I hoped he'd at least remember our arrangement with regard to the license plate. I went into the kitchen to find the maid. She was sitting there at a stainless-steel table gorging on a round cheese with a penknife. She must have assumed the old men were out for the night and had reverted to her post-official-duties state. She stared at me in shock for a moment and then burst out laughing. She was still barefoot and I was still in my sling and dressing gown. I told her that I needed her help, for which I'd slip her a nice tip.

"What kind of help?"

"I don't know yet. Do you know the code to the safe?"

"Of course."

"I don't want anything of his. Just my things."

"Now?"

"No, when the time comes."

I told her to come up to my room in five minutes and get the tip. She could keep it until I called in the favor.

When she arrived at my door I gave her three twenty-dollar bills from the money she had returned to me from the safe and told her not to tell the doctor. I locked the door behind me and waited. The doctor did not call out or come looking for me. Probably, I thought, the maid took him to bed every night after he had emptied one of his bottles of Duhart-Milon and then amused herself alone in the house as if she were its nocturnal mistress. It made no difference to me either way; it was none of my business. Who was Hansel and who was Gretel? The only reason to get married would be to avoid a lingering twilight with a contemptuous maid—but then again it was what he wanted and I couldn't argue with that. He had not adequately explained why he had taken me in, and the longer I thought about it the less I was able to believe his own expressions of doctorly duty. The Hippocratic Oath didn't usually extend to strangers found in hammocks. Maybe he was just amusing himself: a random meeting on the road and he had done it on a whim. But then, why the safe? It was then that I saw that a small container of Valium tablets had been set on my night table next to a glass of water. It was a thoughtful touch, as casual as bedside chocolate mints, and I took two to numb the pain in my arm and try to sleep. But in the end, I hardly slept at all. In the hills behind us, the calls of the coyotes swept as echoes down the valleys and the ravine until they filled my room with a sound of bedlam.

SEVENTEEN

LATE IN THE AFTERNOON THE FOLLOWING DAY, AS I lay in my room, I heard the front bell ring and the maid making her way quietly down the path to the gates. She had let in a visitor, I assumed, and from the window I could see a section of the path that snaked through the garden.

Down this path came a uniformed policeman. He took off his hat and tucked it under one arm. They went into the house and soon the sound of the male voices echoed up to my corridor. There was some polite laughter and a music of glasses. He only stayed about ten minutes, and at the end of his term he was escorted back up the garden path by the maid. A heavyset middle-aged official whom the doctor had obviously been socially lubricating for many years. A man likely easy to sway and charm, willing to share a shot and a bit of gossip. As the gate closed behind him I heard his car start up—a driver had been waiting for him—and a puff of road dust rose up slowly above the wall.

I was already thinking of getting out that morning. You always know when you are being held against your will, even if the people doing it are nice as nuns. It wasn't a strong sense of duty toward my clients; I no longer much believed in their indignation or the worthiness of their cause. All I felt now was a need to confront the Zinns and make them pay for their arrogance. It was the arrogance of the age, it seemed to me, the insolence of easy money, and a little bit of vengeance would do them both good. The thought of it suddenly made me feel better. A kick in the teeth, a comeuppance was what they needed, and tracking them down from now on would be pure pleasure. May you watch the bodies of your enemies float past you on the river.

I went down for a walk in the garden and to my surprise couldn't find the doctor anywhere. I wandered as far as the back wall, behind which the mountains rose into a sky that made me think of the high-altitude atmosphere over Mexico City back in the days when the air was clear. The air seven thousand feet up that makes Popocatépetl seem closer than it is.

At dusk the maid found me still sitting in the garden. She was sly and discreet now that money had changed hands between us.

"We had a visit earlier," she said, after offering to bring me some tea. "A state policeman whom El Doctor plays cards with on Sunday nights. They talked about you."

"I'll bet they did."

"But nothing will happen. Relax."

She seemed to be wondering what I would do. Jump over the wall—dance flamenco . . .

"You and El Doctor will eat outside at six. Do you want to go for a swim? You'll have to keep your arm dry."

"If I do, I'll drown."

At dinner the doctor was in a wheelchair for some reason, and although he complained about his decaying legs he was in good spirits and ready to tease me with his new information.

"You'll be interested to know," he said with some baffling grandness, "that the car you are looking for has been traced to an owner in San Miguel de Allende. I suppose you'd like to know what the owner's name is?"

Jesús Aguayo. He was domiciled in a small town near San Miguel called Atotonilco el Grande.

"I can't say who he is, but this is who the car belongs to. I wouldn't advise you to go looking for it, though."

"It's very good advice."

"The police, I'm afraid, have gotten wind of what happened down in Cuastecomates. I am going to have to ask you to stay in the house for a few days while we sort it out. I can't be party to a crime while it's being investigated, can I? There's no need to get excited. You can stay here and get better while it's being looked into."

This was bad news, but I kept a lid on my alarm. It was a form of house arrest, then, but there was no one to enforce it but the maid. I had done well to bribe her and bring her over to my side.

"It's very kind of you. I'm feeling better already."

"You're a very curious man, Waldstein. What kind of name is that, anyway? Are you German?"

"I might have been in a previous life."

"Oh, that might have been unpleasant. You should go to a clairvoyant."

"It has crossed my mind."

"Maybe that's why you're so tough?"

We ate on and the subject was gradually dropped. But

now I had to rethink. I needed to hunt down Jesús Aguayo and I needed to do it slyly. I played chess with the doctor after dinner and the hours went by in quiet talk about gardens and investments and some of our old cases. He brought up the latter and I told him, on the spur of the moment, that every case felt, in some ways, like a fairy tale. A story being concocted by a higher power that sucked one in, forcing one to obey its demented laws. The maid then wheeled him out to a terrace at the back of the garden and we sat there in a summer house smoking cigars and looking down at a primeval landscape of manzanilla oaks and trees I didn't know spread across canyons and thorned hillsides. There was so sign of a road or of the sea. We took our coffee there and the doctor apologized for asking me not to leave the house. As I could see, he added, there would be nowhere for me to go anyway, and now I understood why he had brought me to that spot. He explained mildly that a dirt track went to the bottom of the mountain and it was about five miles on rough stones. The local people walked it, but I was not a local person.

"I wonder what you meant by saying every case was a fairy tale," he said. "You mean it didn't seem real?"

"Each one felt like a story being told by someone else. It's a wild feeling one gets. One thing leads to another, but later you can't remember how it all pieced together."

"Does it make any sense being here now?"

"None."

He let his chuckle play out for all it was worth.

———

SOON HE HAD fallen asleep again. The maid came silently across the lawns with a metal lantern with a candle inside it. She set it down on the stone garden table before us and gathered up the emptied glasses and the extinguished cigars. I asked her if he fell asleep like this every night. She said he was getting ready for death, and that she added a little sedative to his drink every night to ease him into sleep. Almost immediately, moths began to swirl around the lantern and from behind them she looked down at me with a cold indecision. She began to smile. Since her employer was now unconscious I asked her about the policeman's visit. Oh, she said, she had listened to the whole thing from the kitchen while they were sharing a *fino*.

The cop had told Quiñones that the quantity of blood at the scene of the abandoned house had aroused their interest, but not yet their solid suspicions. He had wanted to know who I was. "I have no idea," El Doctor had said.

"So he's a stranger who your man picked up from Dr. Abrego that night? And he had been found at the hotel in Cuastecomates?"

That was how they had talked.

"The policeman told the doctor to keep you here until he has dug around a bit. They think you are not telling the truth."

"Is that right?"

I tried to sound as indignant as I could.

"That's what they said," she drawled.

"I think I should leave tonight, if I can. I can walk down the track—is it five miles?"

161

"A little less, but you'll be able to manage it." But she looked unsure.

"Is there a village where I can catch a bus tomorrow morning?"

"Where are you going?"

"I'm going to head down south to San Miguel de Allende."

"Right at the road, they have buses that go to Ciudad Guzmán."

It was then two hours before midnight. I said I would come down again from my room at two in the morning. The doctor would be in his nightly coma and she had all the keys to the property. I walked with her back to the house as she pushed the wheelchair ahead of her, and from the fortress came the calls of birds that I hadn't heard during the day. I asked her what she did with her nights. She drank alone in the magnificent house and played jazz. She was saving up to go home with enough money to buy a shop. It was a plan, at least. It was more than I had. I went upstairs and dressed in my own clothes for the first time since arriving there, then waited for the appointed hour.

She came up to the room before that with my money and the cane from the safe, true to her word. In the kitchen she made me coffee and a sandwich for the road.

"What will you tell the doctor?"

"I'll say you disappeared without a trace while I was sleeping."

AT TWO SHE took me up to the gate, unlocked it, and saw me out onto the rocky dirt road. I had nothing with me except

162

money and the cane. I didn't know what to say to her: it was a kindness that an old man wouldn't forget. As I picked my way down the road, she stood at the gate watching me until I passed out of sight. It must have given her some kind of small satisfaction. Left alone with no bag, but without a shred of anxiety about it, I walked through the remainder of the night in a cool air, the yucca on the hills around me forming what looked like a vast nave of votive flowers. The sky was suddenly dramatized by a nervous, uncertain moonlight, by which the shapes of things became more and more unknown, and by its light I found the little road that led to the neighboring village.

EIGHTEEN

I T WAS A DUSTY FARM TOWN WITH TRACTORS PARKED IN the alleys and jacaranda trees serving as shelters for donkeys. The trees lent the animals a pale-lavender tint as light returned to the world, and I found the bus stop with benches where a few old ladies were already gathered. I asked about the bus to Ciudad Guzmán. It would come at seven. I sat on one of the benches and emptied a coconut I had bought at a store on the square, then wondered how much the maid would lie for me when El Doctor woke up and demanded to know where I was. But the bus came at seven with no incident. I sat at the back and no one shot a glance at me and my exotic sling. I asked the driver if I could change in Guzmán for another bus to San Miguel. *Claro que si.*

The mood on the bus was jovial. Before we left, a small boy came down the aisles and placed a paper image of the Virgin of Guadalupe on each passenger's knee. A protection against traffic accidents.

All morning I slept again.

When I was jolted awake, we were sailing like children on a school trip through apricot groves and hills of maize and villages filled with closed hotels and cantinas where the televisions were never turned off.

The road went through valleys of cactus, upon whose heads hundreds of crows sat as if waiting for their morning sun. It ran through a quiet valley of golden prickly poppies. On either side stood ocher churches with skulls and cross-bones cemented into their façades. The milpas bursting with fresh corn, rising toward crests of rock. The dogs stirred as the bus swept past them, opening their jaws for a moment. As the agave farms petered out, the fields were charred, smoking, men beating the fires as they labored across them.

The road curved in places with operatic courage through slopes of *flor de izote* and shaving brush trees. The flower heads shone for miles in a high and mighty sun, entire hillsides covered with the miracle.

At Guzmán I went for lunch near the bus station. The heat had returned a little. How good it was to disappear again into a crowd, to drink beer with *tortas*. The bus for San Miguel left in the middle of the afternoon.

At a hotel in San Miguel I asked the front desk to call me a cab to Atotonilco, which was about six miles to the north; for the next half hour I basked in the sun in the hotel courtyard and healed. The wound was beginning to close.

THE TAXI DRIVER parked up in the main square in Atotonilco. The little village was known for its church built shortly after the Spanish conquest, with its high, corroded wooden doors flung open and covered with monochrome frescoes. I went over to a *tiendita* and asked a woman if she had seen a Señor Aguayo that morning.

She knew him because everyone did. There were little

more than six streets in Atotonilco, all of them around the church, and he lived on one of them. It had long red walls and dry, whispering trees. The gates were locked and the house beyond them couldn't be seen beyond the walls. I rang the bell.

When no one came, I rang again.

Before long a maid opened the gate and peered out. I asked where Jesús was.

"He's down at the *grutas* taking a hot swim."

Behind her I saw a low villa with yellow walls and a chained dog panting in the shade.

"A hot swim?"

"It's a hot spring out on the road. You can walk there."

He went there every morning for his rheumatism.

"Are you a friend?" she asked.

I went back to the *tiendita* and asked about the hot spring. It was a half-hour walk on the road, but there was also a short-cut through the woods.

I told the driver to wait in the square and set off.

At first the path cut through fields of wild trees and high weeds, through ruined fragments of houses. On the far side of the woods there was indeed a hot-spring outdoor spa of some kind with steaming pools and what looked like a small hotel. It was deserted. The pools ran into man-made caves where the steam collected, and out in the sunlight there was a deck chair with clothes folded on its back. When I appeared, a boy came out of the trees and asked me if I'd like a day pass for the hot springs and a bathing suit. I got a suit and changed in the open. The horror of the body unseen. The boy brought me an ice water and I went down into the burning water and waded across the pool, keeping my sling raised and dry, toward the grotto.

The caves were built with loose rocks and vaulted high. The water was chest deep and the whole labyrinth was filled with an ultramarine light. I came to a darkened chamber where the steam was intense, and here I found a man of about forty sitting peacefully by himself with a washcloth over his face.

When he sensed my presence he removed the washcloth and sank down and looked over at the stranger.

I stayed by the opposite wall and we stewed for a few minutes. No sound came from the outside world and no new guests had arrived at the spa. It was the moment to ask him if he was Jesús Aguayo.

"Who are you?" he said.

"I'm a friend of the Linders."

"Ah, I see."

He asked me how I knew them.

It was a spiel I had down pat by now. I said I'd heard they'd retired in Mexico and had a house somewhere in the vicinity.

"Sure they do."

"They told me they had a friend here. They gave your name. I went calling on you in Atotonilco and your maid said you were here. So I'm here, too."

"I see."

But his eyes panicked for a moment.

"What happened to your arm?"

"Arthritis. It feels better in a sling."

"Maybe we should go and talk about this outside?"

"Maybe we should talk about it here. It's cozy and I like the steam."

It was jolting the way we smiled at the same time.

"I don't really know the Linders," he went on. "They're friends of friends. I do favors for them when they ask."

"I'd like to know what it is you do for them. Or if you like we can go down to the police station in San Miguel and you can tell them there. I'll tell them there's a white Grand Am parked at your house and it might not matter to them, but then again it might. I'm sure you've been busy with other jobs."

"I have nothing against going down there. But why should I? And, again, who are you?"

"Well, let's just say I lost my car and I'm annoyed about it. Whoever stole it owes me compensation. Rather than involving you, I thought I'd ask Mr. Linder himself. I thought you could take me to his house if I made a donation to you and also forgot about going to the *delegación*. It could be a very simple arrangement, and Mr. Linder would never know it was you. You could just leave me in the road nearby."

"Are you kidding me?"

"Yes, I know I have a funny way of speaking. But actually I'm a really unpleasant person. I don't have any sense of humor at all."

He swore in the Mexican way: *la chingada.*

I suggested he go back to the house, take his car, and return there to pick me up. From here he could drive me to wherever they lived. Where was it, since we had come to the matter?

"I think I should call them first and see what they say."

"You could do that," I said. "Or you could just let it be a surprise. They won't know how I found them."

With their haul from Pacific Mutual, they had found a compound in the hills above Guanajuato, according to him. From there they drove down to the coast for parties and social occasions, and as it was slightly off the beaten track for wealthy Americans they enjoyed more discretion.

"But I'm not taking you there," he insisted.

He said he would call Mrs. Linder and ask her what she wanted to do.

"I'd rather you didn't. If you're scared of them just give me the address and I'll go there on my own."

"Scared?"

Wounded pride flared up and his eyes enlarged to the point of explosion.

"I am scared of no man!"

"Just give me the address and we're quits. I like that you're not scared of a measly little gringo drifter."

"In that case," he said, suddenly placated, "we can just go outside and have a drink. I will write down the address for you. It's fortunate that we are in such a lonely place." .

"It's fortunate I don't have to call the police."

"Ah, you wouldn't call them."

His moods were as quick as those of an English sky.

Outside, we sat on the deck chairs and the waiter brought us lemonades. It was a cheerful resort of some kind, but fallen on hard times or else it had never known good ones. My correspondent was now more at his ease, sure as he was that I would go away and leave him in peace, and he wrote down the address on a postcard that the waiter brought him. To think that I had come all that way to get an address scribbled on a piece of paper. I asked him about the man who had brought the car back to Atotonilco, the man who liked to play with tops, but he had never heard of such a person.

"I do errands for rich people," he said with an uncrooked smile. "I'm just someone who does them small favors. I'm nobody."

He added that he had never met the Linders.

"*El Linder*," he concluded, "*es una fantasma.*"

I glanced down at the card and saw an address on a road not far from the remote church of Mineral del Cedro and a settlement called Calderones. So it was another wild-goose chase to a small *pueblo* or a shaded lane in the middle of nowhere. Another lark for an old man with fading legs. For a moment I wondered if it was worth the time. But then I couldn't stand the idea that the little greasy con man had gotten the better of me and that I couldn't keep up with his cat-and-mouse games. I wanted to see the *fantasma*'s eye light up with a moment of horror, just once. And aside from that, I have a curious dislike for people who try to cripple me, although I often understand their emotions and even more their motives. Motives make more sense than emotions.

NINETEEN

B Y TWO THAT DAY I WAS IN GUANAJUATO IN A CHEAP hotel, tall and narrow, on a street called Cantarranas, the singing frogs. I got a room on the very top floor, so high that the city itself seemed far below me, a city unlike anything I knew: a place shoehorned into a narrow ravine. Its lights and white houses made me think of Bethlehem in long-ago books. At sundown I went down into the streets and had dinner. Through the squares and alleys, students in black capes and masks went in bands strumming mandolins, serenading opportunistically, and it wasn't hard to imagine the Linders having their weekend dinners here.

It was past nine by the time I hailed a taxi and asked him to take me out to the address on the slip of paper. He didn't know it, but he said he would find it without fail and that was good enough for me. It was only a mile out of town, into the mining hills that had once made Madrid the silver capital of Europe. Roads winding into the darkness where the houses of the wealthy stood in isolate grandeur.

The taxi left me at the foot of a sweeping drive flanked with cypresses. He asked me how long I'd be staying and if he should wait. I said he could park for an hour or two out of sight, if he didn't mind; the pay would be good.

I went up the drive. Halfway to a low but capacious hacienda-style villa I heard chatter, music, the terrible noise of merriment and party making. This was not what I had expected. It was too shabby to intrude on a party without a change of clothes. With my bandaged arm, I looked already like a man waiting for the hospital ward from which he wouldn't be leaving. But on the drive itself servants suddenly appeared with welcoming torches and little silk masks with elastic bands. It was a masked affair and the disguises were given out to all arrivals. Just as they saw me, another car drew up at the end of the drive and a party of four got out and followed me toward the house. I decided to tag along with them. They were Americans, two elderly couples in ghastly finery. I have a way of getting on with the ghosts of the past. Did they know Paul and Dolores? Why no, they'd never met them. They'd been invited by mutual friends in San Miguel. The American club in the Central Highlands was wealthy and large. Every year new members appeared, retirees anxious to start a new life, and they were buying all the lovely haciendas in the hills. The Reagan years had been good to them. I introduced myself as Barry Waldstein and we came to a grand columned porch with the masks fixed to our sweating faces. They were Aztec themed, gods and goddesses we didn't know but that made us look like psychotics in the context of butlers holding out flutes.

A house in the hills, servants and tapestries: so this was what the ambitious *fantasma* had managed to procure with his haul. It was as impressive as it was baffling. Its proprietor had been running around on buses just to shake off an old hand like me, while all the time he could have hidden out here and I would not have found him easily. I suddenly realized, then, that I was the only threat to his wonderful new life. Maybe no one else there knew how his chandeliers had been paid for. He was a man on the run; but you'd never know it on that Friday night.

The party spilled out into a magnificent Spanish garden with a tile fountain and more cypress trees, where bars were set up next to a buffet of silver tureens. The crowd was large enough that I could blend in and disappear. I felt the pulse of drugs making their way around the rooms, the quiet drugs of the respectable and the rich that are discreetly laid over the usual cocktails and shots of liquor—and indeed there were two tables devoted solely to mescal and tequila served in artful forms, Italian shot glasses and saucers of pink salt. The men were going at it, roaring with satisfaction and swaying slightly as their nerves began to lose control. Soon a jazz band started up and cocaine appeared nonchalantly on the tables in the remoter rooms inside, spread out over eighteenth-century tables and sucked up by teenagers and fossils alike.

Now I saw how useful the masks must be for the hosts. It was hard to find them, and who knew if they were even there at all. The lights were on in the hacienda's second floor. Perhaps they were up there watching us.

I went into the garden, where a vortex of beautiful women, Americans and locals, swirled together to the strange music of Tina Turner. Between the cypresses, lawns rolled down into the dark, and here and there people lay with paper trays of cake and champagne flutes looking up at the stars. They looked like candy wrappers that had been tossed aside by a giant child. For a moment I wondered where I was, and why

I had come, and yet the shots were there to enjoy as well as canapés and empanadas. I went through the crowd looking for Donald and yet I didn't find him.

I went from room to room. Some of them were painted pink and blue, with trompe-l'oeil marble panels and bookcases that had clearly been there a lot longer than the new owners. I asked around. But was he called Donald or Paul? I tried "Señor Linder" and some said they had seen him earlier giving a speech to his guests.

On one of the long corridors that connected the various parts of the house, its walls hung with modern paintings, a man came up to me and cried, "Norman!" He grabbed my arm, half spinning me around, and behind him appeared a woman who was clearly with him. They were drunk and the masks had begun to slip on their faces. They asked me if I had seen Linder.

"He's around somewhere," I said.

"It's a pain, the way he asks us here and then disappears. What do you think of the house?"

"It's a palace."

"No kidding," the woman said.

"What happened to your arm?"

"Lawn mower accident."

Suddenly the man gave me a second look.

"Say, wait a minute—"

I moved off and they decided to laugh it off.

"I could have sworn that was Norman," the man bawled.

"Leave him be, Roman."

The woman stared after me but I was gone, back into the smoke and the crush of bodies. I came out into the main hallway and it was curiously deserted but for the maids and waiters who had obviously been hired only for the evening. From there a grand spiral staircase rose to the second floor like something from *Gone with the Wind*. No one minded me going up it. The corridors here were hushed and the rooms still submerged in their privacy. I looked behind myself down at the hall and noticed one of the waiters staring up at me in confusion. I put a finger to my lips and he melted away. The inoffensive fossil look gets me off a number of hooks these days. I plunged into the first corridor and saw that there were lights under the doors. If anyone stopped me I'd say I was drunk and looking for the bathroom. Soon I could hear voices behind the doors. A man and a woman talking. Their tempers were rising, the man was already shouting. There was the resounding sound of a smack to the face. The woman sobbed. The man shouted a few vile things. He stormed about. Suddenly one of the doors snapped open and a masked male head popped into the corridor's darkness and the eyes revealed by the slits glittered with a mixture of fathomless anger and disequilibrium.

"Who's there?" he barked, and saw only me tottering with an outstretched hand (I had left the cane downstairs with the staff). A woman appeared behind him and asked who and what it was.

"Do I know you?" the man barked again.

"I was looking for the bathroom," I said.

The man turned back into the room and his tone was acid.

"He says he's looking for the john. No, he's not drunk."

"But I am," I corrected him.

He gave me a second look and the purple mask he was wearing seemed to shine brighter with its silver sequins.

"There's one at the other end of the landing, old sport. Don't fall down the stairs on the way."

"I'll show him," the woman said, and I recognized her voice at once.

"No, leave him be. It doesn't have to be a humiliation."

"I can go."

"Shut up, and sit down. I'm not in the mood for a conference."

"I'll find it," I said, muffling my own voice and retreating back to the stairs. The woman stepped out into the corridor and watched me go. My voice, she must have recognized my voice. But they were also tipsy, their voices slurred and slippery. They had the high-wire arrogance of the intoxicated.

I went back down the stairs and waited in the garden. So I had found them alone in their bedroom where they were probably doing lines of coke by themselves. I no longer had my miniature camera, of course, but I went from room to room then, making a mental inventory of everything in them. Antique furniture, rugs, mirrors, modern paintings, glassware, jade Indian art, the loots of continents and centuries assembled hastily by amateurs. It was a palace filled by magpies.

It was a little after ten, and so in their terms the night was still young. I decided to ask a young lady to dance, and seeing my crippled arm and tattered shoes she accepted. Sexual noblesse oblige. We waltzed on the lawn and the hours went by. The stars, however, still held their positions.

It was not yet midnight when I went back into the house,

found a bathroom to lock myself in, and took off the mask. My face had turned red underneath it. I ripped off the elastic band, then went back out into the hallway and collared one of the waiters. Showing him the broken mask, I asked for a replacement.

The new one was dark green and gave me a fresh look, and I ventured out again a new man. In the main salon, a crowd gathered around a grand piano and there the mask from the room upstairs, easily recognizable, was seated to play. He was belting out some Artie Shaw number which I recognized, and it was only a few bars in that I realized it was "Blues in the Night." But how was it that he knew it as well and could play it so comfortably? I sat down to listen and began to feel cold all over. From across the room, the player looked tall and slim, athletic almost, a suave impersonator from someone else's nightmare. Why was he playing music from the forties? Then I remembered that he was almost the same age as I was, and there was no reason why he shouldn't. I got up and went out into the garden. A few minutes later he came out as well, surrounded by a gaggle of women. They hadn't noticed me seated in a gazebo and went to the pool that lay adjacent to a terrace and sat down on the grass around it. I waited until they had settled down, then quietly joined them. There was no sign of the wife. The man who appeared to be our host lay sprawled among his beauties, smoking from a cigarette holder and exposing the black socks he wore under his slippers. And here was the astonishing thing: they were dark-blue velvet Alberts with gold crown embroideries, just like the doctor's. Linder wore them, however, with greater effect and they seemed to work as certificates of his success. I sat

177

down behind him, unnoticed at first, and observed the white hair that the elastic strap of his mask traversed. I was sure it was Donald. But then, the *fantasma* had nothing solid about him. He was made of air. Nevertheless, sensing my presence, he turned suddenly and smiled. He hadn't even seen me; it was a fish sensing another fish using its lateral line. He leaned forward and as he did I could see his chin below the mask; it had the tense set of the cruel and feckless. He was onto me, and in some way he didn't mind. Perhaps it was even more of a game to him than it was to me.

TWENTY

"SO YOU FOUND THE RESTROOM, I ASSUME. I WAS WOR-ried about you. Ah, the bladders of the old. But here you are again." His voice was that of a female opera singer on a night off, a voice smoothed with lavender oil and just as high as it had been when I had first heard it. "You changed your mask, but your shoes are the same." He laughed. "Can we get you a drink?"

"I'll have a shot if you're having one."

The waiters around us sprang into life.

"Get the man a shot and one for me, too. *Dos shots*, okay?"

Nothing surprised me about him yet; the phantom I had been chasing for days was now in front of me without any fanfare. He wasn't extraordinary at all. His California accent, his expensive seven-fold tie were all as simple as pieces of clockwork in a mechanism that ticked and performed their functions. It was incredible that he was the con that he was, but his physical presence wasn't larger than life. He even looked a little small. But then I remembered what Dolores had said about his blue eyes and I found that they were indeed the blue of minerals from deep in the earth, and terrible because of it. He spoke a few words to the women and, magically dismissed, they melted away into the larger party. He sat up and suggested we sit on the metal chairs at the edge of the terrace. He asked my name. I said I was Norman Petty. He said he was Paul. He also admitted that he was the host and that it was funny that I didn't know that.

"Of course I don't know everyone here," he said affably as we relocated. "I don't think I know you. Were you invited by a friend?"

"I came with Roman."

"Ah, Roman. So you know Roman? I loathe Roman myself, but my wife always insists on inviting him. How do you know him?"

Now was a throw of the dice, but it had to be done.

"I met him on a yacht down in Manzanillo."

"There you go. Everyone meets everyone on those damned yachts. I swear to God we even look the same these days. Do you fish, Norman?"

"I'm a marlin man myself. How about you?"

"There's no point being anything else!"

The shots came on a tray and we knocked them back. A second round was poured.

"I do like slugging shots with a stranger," he said. "It's so refreshing. You get so tired of the people you already know."

He added that he was happy to get away from his wife for a while.

"She's a terrible harpy, Norman. Why do we always marry harpies? Or do we make them into harpies? I can't tell anymore."

"Maybe it's us who are the harpies."

"Quite true, Norman, quite true. Now tell me, where do you like to fish marlin?"

"I go to Mazatlán, like everyone else."

"It's the best."

"It's the best place in Mexico for marlin."

"That it is. But Guanajuato has the air. Don't you love the air here? I guess you must be retired here, like us."

"I'm just looking for a house here, actually."

"Are you now? Well, you've come to the right place."

We sank the second round and he asked me if I liked to smoke weed. It was one of his hobbies and he had a veritable library of the stuff. But I passed. I said it always made me too courteous. He looked up toward the house and his mouth grew harder. He wanted to know what line of business I was in, and I said that once upon a time I had been a newspaper reporter for a paper in New Jersey. After that, I had retired and taken up ikebana. That was Japanese flower arranging.

"No shit," he murmured.

Yes, I said, I found it relaxed me during my empty hours. I hated flowers, but I loved ikebana. Had he ever tried it? It was a shame he hadn't. Now that he was retired—

"I didn't say I was retired," he smiled. "What gives you that idea?"

"It's a hell of a place to be working from."

"Well, all right, we're retired, since you mention it. Say, Norman, what do you think I paid for this pile?"

"That's a tough one—a million?"

"Damn good guess. But why do you assume we bought it?"

The accent was becoming even clearer now: the desert Californian townlets, the air bases, the monotonous irrigated farmlands and the border saloons. According to my researches, his father had run a flour refinery back in the day. They say the flour would sometimes combust in the warehouses and make explosions that sounded like bombs in the middle of the El Centro nights. I'd forgotten who had told me that. It wasn't Bonhoeffer. Perhaps I remembered it myself.

"I didn't assume a thing," I said, as coldly as I could.

"It's just as well. So you came with Roman? Shame we can't find him and have him over for a drink. Do you loathe him as much as I do?"

He called over one of the automata.

"Go and see if you can find Señor Roman for me. A friend here who wants to invite him for a drink."

"Yes, Señor."

He turned back to me:

"Never could learn the damn language. It just gets on top of me and smothers me."

"You should try Indonesian."

"Well, I won't be going to Indonesia anytime soon."

"I wonder what brought you here, then."

He stretched his legs and tiny slivers of white shin appeared above his socks.

"I like it down here. Don't you?"

He broke into a grin that offered, to my surprise, no malice whatsoever.

"I might even get a place," I said. "Do you know one for sale?"

"I'll ask Roman when he comes. He knows all about that sort of thing."

Yes, the elusive Roman. It was now that I had to get out of

there before it was too late. I tried a glance at the watch, but he wasn't buying it.

"You can't leave now," he said. "Not when Roman is about to join us. He'll get upset and cry."

By the way, he added, what had happened to my arm?

"Lawn mower accident."

"You should go see an American doctor. I think they've patched you up wrong."

"Patched is patched."

"You know what Mikhail Kalashnikov used to say? He said, 'I wish I'd invented a lawn mower.' He said that having invented the world's most famous automatic rifle sometimes made him sad and he wished he'd invented something more useful. Something to mow the lawn. See what I mean?"

He looked up and over my shoulder, and all the cruelty came back into his blue eyes. I turned. It was Roman, unfortunately, escorted by the waiter and without his wife, and there was something nervous and disagreeable about the way he carried himself, as if he had been hustled down there against his will. Looking over at me he at first didn't recognize the changed mask, but the arm in its sling jolted his memory and he remembered our little meeting in the corridor all those hours ago, now perceived from the far side of a wall of drugs and alcohol.

"Oh," he said.

"Sit down, Roman. I believe you know our masked friend here. Norman's been telling me all about himself. I told him that maybe you can help find him a house out here. Roman is our local real estate shark. Aren't you, Roman?"

"I don't know about that."

He sat, but he had already given me the mocking eye.

"I'm glad you invited Norman," Donald said. "Because otherwise I wouldn't meet any new faces. And I always like to meet a new face."

"I invited Norman, but I'm not sure—"

The three of us in our masks were so absurd that I couldn't help a quick laugh.

"We look like the Three Musketeers," I said.

"What are you not sure about, Roman?"

"At first I thought—he looked like Norman. But now I'm not so sure."

"Not sure?"

"He's got a mask on, hasn't he?"

"You can see through a mask. Roman here seems to think you might not be Norman. Isn't that funny? Maybe you should take your mask off and we can determine the matter. I'd say that was a fine idea at this point. I'm sure Norman would agree if he was here."

"I thought there were rules about that."

"But if Roman isn't sure that you're Norman, neither am I."

Roman tried to laugh his way through it.

"Come on, it's not a big deal. Maybe he is Norman and he just sounds different. I don't care if he is or not. Hey, buddy, if you say you're Norman, you are."

"I don't want complete strangers wandering around my house calling themselves Norman. Either they're Norman or they're not. Friends of friends only."

"But I am a friend of a friend."

"Oh?"

I straightened myself up and gave him the eye.

"I'm a friend of Paul Linder. I believe you know him, too."

Not understanding, Roman prolonged his chimplike grin.

"That's funny."

"You know," Donald said, his legs uncoiling slightly in their velvet slippers. "It's been a long evening and sometimes we have to bring long evenings to an end. It gets confusing after a while. Maybe you should tell us what your real name is and we can leave it at that. We can call you a taxi if you'd prefer."

Two men were walking across the lawn toward us, and they weren't Boy Scouts running to the rescue.

"Is that the departure committee?"

"They're the departure boys, yes. But I'd like to know your name first."

"Philip. Do you know any other Philips?"

"I don't understand," Roman protested.

Donald turned to him.

"You don't know him and neither do I. Are you out of your fucking mind?"

I got to my feet before the Boy Scouts arrived, but I wanted to ask him before I was hurled out of paradise how he knew Paul Linder and what he had done with him. But there wouldn't be time.

"Paul was a nice guy," I said. "Last time I looked. But the funny thing is he disappeared. They say people can't disappear."

"Disappeared?" Roman cried, staring, I supposed, at the only Paul Linder he knew or would ever know.

"You're drunk," Donald said, "but I don't mind. *Muchachos*, get him out of here."

"You shouldn't say *muchachos*. It sounds wrong."

"I'll say whatever I want. Shall we go out together, Mr. Philip?"

"I'd be delighted."

We left Roman there and the four of us struggled through the dancing couples on the lawn. Inside the throng I met the girl I had danced with before, much more stoned, and I stepped out of the prison of my body for a moment and twirled her around with my good arm. Astonished, my escort couldn't intervene without making an awkward scene and so had to let us dance. Then one of the Scouts grabbed my gammy arm and twisted it a little so that the pain shot across my torso. It was a way of hastening my steps. We came out into the porch, the moonlight gilding the driveway. El Donaldo then dared to speak up at me.

"You come here, expecting me to pay you off—you piece of trash. You don't take a hint, do you?"

He held back then and the Scout who had my arm suddenly threw me to the ground, watching me roll over like a barrel and then come to a stop by the driveway's whitewashed curb.

"I should have them finish it," the master called down to me. "I could have them cut off your hands and roll you into a ditch. Who would find you, you little prick?"

Why don't you, I thought. It would be the easiest thing and I wouldn't be the one who would care the most. But I knew why then he didn't—not there, not on that evening. He didn't want another thing to cover up, and already there had been too many witnesses. I picked myself up and walked down toward the pompous colonial gates.

"Hey, Philip," he called after me. "Fuck you and fuck your ways."

Then something clattered behind me—it was the cane that I had forgotten and which the Scout had thrown after me. It was worth picking up, and as I did so I gave them what I thought was a proud look.

"You can walk back to Guanajuato," he called again. "Get drunk somewhere, you piece of old shit. It's the only thing you can do well."

They stood there waiting for me to pass through their gate. Then, as soon as I was on the road, the rush of that evening hit me. It was over, the shenanigans and the cat-and-mouse; I was still alive and only slightly bruised. I knew then that I was through with this jaunt: that it was an ordeal for nothing, a trip for biscuits. It was a thought that had circled in my mind for a while now, like a stone rolling downhill, it was a certainty that would take me with it.

The hills were lit up by the moon and the nightjars were singing. At the bend of the road below me the taxi driver was waiting, and had been for hours. I couldn't think what had inspired such loyalty, it couldn't have been just money. He even waved to me. I was saved. I called down to him that he was a fool.

"*Che rechulo mi tarzan!*" he shouted back.

I walked slowly down to him and everything around me faded and then glowed brightly again. I expected Donald and his goons to come after me, but instead when I got to the car the driver gestured behind me.

187

I turned to see a woman coming down the road. She had taken off her mask and I saw at once it was Dolores. She was not mad or agitated. She walked alongside the car, and when she was almost next to me she looked back to make sure she hadn't been followed.

"Philip, wait."

I would have rushed her off at this point, and I really should have given her the high hat. She'd been standing by while the goons manhandled an old man. But all the same I had admit to myself that I couldn't turn her away. She looked so confused and wild, which was not her usual look, and there was an entrapment in her expression that made me realize that she was not in command of anything. Not at all. In fact she seemed to be deciding what to do next, biting her lip, her eyes panicking because she had only a few seconds to form a plan. But it was also something else. I thought that she looked magnificently unglamorous that night, as if she had been stripped down to her essential elements by her own fear. Then I recalled the bruise on her neck. I realized suddenly that I had not put it all together before. It was the girl from the slums who was putting up with a life like this because she had nothing to go back to. She was the one fighting her own war against unpleasant men like Donald her whole life and gradually scoring a few secretive victories along the way. I had merely stumbled into that war without understanding it.

"I didn't ask him for money," I protested. "I didn't ask for anything. I just wanted to say good-bye."

My smile didn't provoke one in return.

"And now?" she said.

"I'm out. I know a nice spa on the coast. Look, it's been a real pleasure and all that—"

"No, wait."

Her voice wasn't pleading, but it was halfway there.

"Meet me tomorrow at the Mummy Museum, the cemetery at the back, at three o'clock. I'll bring you what is due you—I promise—and explain everything."

She turned away as I rolled into the car. The headlights swept over her slender form as she walked back briskly to the house where, if she was lucky, no one had missed her.

TWENTY-ONE

I SPENT A DRY AND DREAMLESS NIGHT IN THE CANTAR-
ranas after a meal of tamales and green salsa, and I couldn't
stop thinking about the desperation in Dolores's face the
previous night. She must have risked quite a bit to come
tumbling down the hill after me just for a rare moment of
frankness. But now I got to meet her alone one last time,
and it was a more potent prospect than either going home or
providing evidence for Pacific Mutual. I wondered even then
why I wasn't more suspicious of her, but it's an animal sense:
when someone is not a danger to you, you feel it under your
skin. This left me free to indulge my morbid curiosities. I am
pulled along by the mystery. It cannot be otherwise.

The following afternoon I took a streetcar up the long hill
to the Museo de las Momias. It stood high above the city at
the top of a threadbare hill, with turnstiles outside and tourist
advertisements. It was dedicated to scores of naturally occur-
ring mummies whose bodies had been preserved by dense
nitrates in the local soil, and as such it proved a popular place
for school tours. I wandered on into a cemetery filled with
thin jacaranda trees, frail and sad in a silent sun, and waited
for Dolores.

The trees were filled with rags that rattled in the wind

like Buddhist prayer flags, and the graves were turned a faint blue by the fragments of blossom clinging desperately to the branches. Tombs of archangels and celestial creatures blowing trumpets, but with a hidden strain of Aztec terror. No wonder the French had shriveled up here and turned into mummies. A dust-dry wind swept through it, stirring the plastic rags, and the blue petals were whipped up into little pretty tornadoes and then dumped back on the surfaces of the tombs. She had chosen her spot well.

I only had to wait here on a bench and soak in some sun. A tour group passed through the cemetery with perfunctory distaste, and when Dolores finally appeared we were all but alone.

She was dressed as if for a funeral, in a wide black hat and matching heels. It was as if she had made some small effort for me, a man who couldn't possibly interest her romantically. But she had bothered all the same. She came down an aisle between monumental tombs under the jacarandas and it was as if the previous evening had happened in another life. She carried a small suitcase with her and I knew at once that it was the money she had promised me at Las Hadas but which they had tried to avoid paying before. So she had had a change of heart.

"Shall we go for a walk?" she said.

Like father and stray daughter, we went slowly through the avenues of dead bourgeoisie, while she apologized for everything that had happened.

"I'm sorry about your arm, and the way they treated you last night. There was nothing I could do."

She said her husband was a wild card when he was afraid

of losing everything. And that might include her. I also had been a little rash.

"What's in the suitcase?"

"It's what we agreed on. I think you should take it and be on your way now. Are we agreed?"

"It's fair."

She handed me the suitcase and I was, against all my scruples, glad to have it. By now I had paid for it after all.

"You can stop pretending to be so moral now," she said. "Everything in the world is just money. Look at these tombs. They're all about money, too."

"I never said it wasn't."

"But you don't believe it. You have your honor. Luckily Donald and I don't have any such hindrance."

This wasn't entirely true; my honor was sometimes a sentimental garb to cover other things. I wasn't feeling honorable toward her, anyway. It was the physical grace that swayed everything inside, a wind through bending willows.

"That said," I pointed out, "it does seem a lot of trouble to go to just to avoid bankruptcy. There must be easier ways to enjoy oysters every day for the rest of your life."

"Not at all. Bankruptcy would have been the end of it. I'd say anything was worth it to have a new life. We *do* have a new life. The only problem is you. I mean, the only problem *was* you."

"You certainly bought a nice house."

"Oh, we didn't buy anything. It's a rental. We'll be gone by tomorrow. You won't find us a third time, I can assure you."

She was possibly lying about the rental. I couldn't tell. I held up the suitcase, and it was heavy. They had paid their money, and I had to admit that I felt a moment's disappointment that she hadn't struck out for more. She herself was *worth* more than a simple payout to an old man.

"I should be ashamed to accept this. But I'm not."

"Don't be. We're the same, you and I."

Her eyes were even lovelier under the flowering trees, even more deliciously unstable and oblique, as if she couldn't help them being as they were—eyes making their way through the world just for fun and mischief. I felt a moment's envy for Donald. With all his coarseness and banality, he didn't deserve her. It's what every jealous man from the beginning of time has thought, and almost every one of them has been wrong. But they didn't care any more than I did then.

"You may be right," I said. "I'll go down into town after this and buy myself a suit. I can't deny it'll be pleasant."

"All the same, I don't really understand you."

She said I struck her as a classic lost soul, a pathless wanderer moving from day to day without any deeper purpose. Was that what old age was like, in the end? You didn't care?

"It's not that I don't care."

"Then what is it?"

I said, "I just wanted one last outing. Every man does. One last play at the tables—it's a common wish."

"That's something I don't understand at all."

"But you're young. And you already played your last hand at the table."

"You don't know it's the last. Still, I see what you mean. Maybe I'll get to that point later."

I thought then that I really didn't know anything about

her. And nor did Donald, probably. Who was she? A girl he picked up in a bar in Mazatlán. But that meant nothing. I regretted not looking into it more when I had been there. I could have asked her then, but it was ungentlemanly and would have spoiled the mood. Moods are not things you toss aside thoughtlessly. They're as precious as anything else, and equally fragile.

So I skipped that question and just enjoyed her presence. She was the only thread I was handling as I groped my way through the dark on my small and wind-swept odyssey. A thread as soft as silk, shiny and mysterious; or, if you want to put it another way, a dance partner that is different with every step. Count me as one of those who know that life is unbearable not because it's a tragedy but because it's a romance. Old age only makes it worse, because now the race against time has reached the hour of high noon.

She asked me what I was going to do now, and I said I'd probably go for dinner after my visit to the tailor and then book a flight back to Tijuana. I'd stay at home for a few days to recover and then drive up to see the spooks at Pacific Mutual and tell them I'd found nothing, to my infinite regret.

"They didn't offer you a bounty if you found us, did they?"

"They did, but you paid me more so I won't want to collect it. You can stop worrying. And you?"

"We'll head south, as people always do. Latin America is big enough. If Mexico doesn't work out we'll go to Panama, or some such. You won't follow us to Panama, will you?"

"I've already been, and Panama and I had nothing to say to each other."

"I'm glad to hear that."

"Maybe you should consider getting a divorce there—I hear it's easy."

"Divorce Panama-style. Sounds like an adventure."

For a moment, as we walked like that side by side, I considered something fantastical: asking her to have a late lunch or an early dinner with me. But the idea came and went in the space of a single second. Yet I would have liked to sit across a table from her and talk. I had the feeling she had led quite a life and never told it to anyone yet, at least not to her husband. All she had revealed about herself was the Santa Muerte in the slums of Mazatlán.

We came to a panorama of the city and stood in the sun for a while; I couldn't think of clever things to say. I certainly didn't want it to be the last time I ever saw her. It seemed a waste of a possible enchantment, at least on my side. But she would walk away now, and I would go and order my suit so that two days later I would no longer look like a refugee from a world war.

"We should say good-bye now. I hope you'll accept my apology for all the unfortunate things that have happened. Like I said—"

"It wasn't you."

"No, it wasn't. It's a shame. But lots of things are a shame and we get over them." She smiled brilliantly and took my hand for a moment.

It made me suddenly happy, that tone. That dismissal of the boisterous monster in her life.

"Sayonara, then," I said, and let go of her hand.

"Sayonara, Mr. Marlowe. Watch your step on the way down. People fall over and kill themselves all the time."

"And I only have three lives left."

She watched me go, and when I turned to give her one last look by the turnstiles I couldn't find her in the crowd. Even her tilted elegant hat could not be seen. I went down to the streetcar stop and something burst at the seams of the heart, I couldn't say what. It was as if I had said good-bye to a whole lifetime of women and missed loves and failed connections. No matter. The streetcars keep coming. Sometimes, though, you board them with suitcases filled with thousands of dollars and your mood is not as melancholy as it might have been. However, never had I felt so indifferent to money.

TWENTY-TWO

ON MY BED AT THE CANTARRANAS I OPENED THE SUIT-case and counted out the money until it matched exactly the sum we had agreed on at the Las Hadas. She had kept her word and she must have been glad to buy me off once and for all. I went to a tailor near the hotel later in the evening and ordered two suits, a summer one and a dark one, along with a handsome shoulder bag, and then went to Tasca de los Santos for a long dinner of *fabada* and beer in the shadow of a sherbet-orange church. I spent most of the evening there alone, faced with the inevitable prospect of finally returning home, where I would have to look retirement, and therefore slow decline, in the eyes. Here I was alive and on the make, not yet senile and not yet shelved. But there was only curiosity and it was not enough.

When I came back to the Cantarranas at twelve, the man at the night desk explained that someone had been to the hotel to see me, but that I had not been there and he had turned him away. If I was expecting visitors, it would be better to inform him beforehand and he could relay their messages to me.

"I wasn't expecting anyone," I said.

"But the gentleman was expecting you."

It wasn't quite the same thing, was it?

I told him to call me if my visitor returned. From there I went up to my room, locked the door, and laid a chair against the handle. Then I went to the window, opened it, and sat on the ledge with a glass of Sauza, waiting for my visitor.

But no one came and I lay on the bed, drifting into sleep. The shrill ring of the telephone woke me. I went back to the window with the lights off and saw the visitor emerge into the street, step back from the building, and look up at my window. I recognized him at once, like a specter from a distant dream. It was the man who liked tops, as I had imagined. But I had never really discovered who he was exactly and who was sending him hither and thither, or even why. But now it finally dawned on me that he was working for himself, as we all are in the end. He had figured out a way to make some easy money. I drew back before he saw me. He walked across the street and dove into a small cantina at the corner. He had likely been hiding there all the time. I went back to the bed, picked up the cane, and opened the blade a little.

This time he crossed back to the hotel half an hour later and the phone did not ring. I lifted the chair from the door and opened it slightly and then turned off the light and sat on the bed.

His footsteps came up the creaky old stairs and then along the equally decrepit corridor of the top floor. When he was halfway along it, he sensed that something was wrong and stopped. He had seen the door slightly ajar and the darkness inside the room. Nevertheless he had come that far. As he approached the door and his shadow fell across the threshold, I spoke, without alarm: "Come in, it's a party of two."

He pushed in the door quickly with his foot and the arc of light from the corridor revealed me seated on the bed and the unmistakable premonition of disaster carried in my good hand. He took a step back and swung out of view and I almost unsheathed the blade the whole way, but drawing blood would have awakened all the old ladies who like to call the authorities.

"It's a funny way to meet again," he said from the corridor.

"Why don't you come in?"

He thought about it, and then stepped into the room with the ginger steps of a ballerina.

"Want to sit and have a drink?"

"I'll stay like I am if it's all the same to you."

"Suit yourself. They're your feet."

The suitcase was laid against the wall on the far side of the bed. He said he had come for that and he didn't want anything else from me.

"You came at the wrong time, Topper. I was about to go to bed and have dreams about Rita Hayworth. It's a shame you showed up. You're going away empty-handed tonight and in the morning I'll have my usual breakfast. It'll be swell all round."

"Says who?"

"It'd be a silly thing to knock me out and try to get out of here. I've paid off the guys downstairs and they'd remember you in a heartbeat. So relax. Wipe that sweat off your face. You're too much of a lug for your own good. I wish you'd sit down and we can play cards. No? Like I said, suit yourself."

The sweat was indeed dripping off him. It fell to the floor and spattered the side of his shoe. The room was boiling.

But suddenly he relented, as if he had done the math in his head and the sums didn't pan out. A cockeyed smile and the schoolboy in him resurfaced.

"Whatever," he said. "We'll do a deal if you like. You can put that stupid samurai sword away. You're not as smart as you think you are."

"Is that right? I was thinking that myself. Well, anyway. Instead of another sordid squabble come for breakfast tomorrow at El Canastillo de Flores. You know it. I'll be there at nine and we can throw insults over eggs."

"Breakfast?"

"Yeah, you've heard of it? We can discuss our business like grown-ups."

He snorted in disbelief and yet it was a civilized proposition for him. Maybe he wasn't used to those.

I got up and walked slowly to the door, ceremonially opening it wider for him, and he waited for a minute or two weighing his considerable options, then walked back down the corridor to the stairwell. From there, he said, "You won't get to keep any of it. It's mine." But I didn't want it anyway, since it had the stamp of bad luck and evil spirits.

When he had descended to the floor below I came out and stood at the head of the stairs. I called down to him.

"In public, you'll be nicer."

He said nothing, but I knew he'd come the next morning. He carried on descending into the lobby and I went to bed and dreamt of Arctic seals being hunted on ice floes by pods of orcas, the chair still tilted against the door handle.

———

JUST BEFORE CARNIVAL the skies held hints of antimony and silver dust. It was a light that made me feel as if I had downed a quick glass of champagne every time I exited from the shadows of the hotel and strode into the street. The heat of spring swept down from the barren ravines around the city. That morning it was the same.

At daybreak I took half the money out of the suitcase and put it under the mattress. I got to El Canastillo de Flores early with the suitcase and ordered my usual *café de olla* with churros and then, to cap them off, a little shot of brandy to perk me up for a testy meeting. Past a certain age, a single shot at breakfast has no effect. I told the waiter to bring over two plates of huevos rancheros as soon as my guest arrived and a side of mole. Then I sat at an outside table and watched the flowers grow centimeter by centimeter in the flower beds of the Plaza de la Paz, waiting for Topper to come lumbering down to meet his fate. It was right next door to where I had eaten dinner the night before, with the same view of a female statue mounted upon a strange stone sphere. The orange-sherbet cathedral with its dramatic dark lines was now lit by the sun and the doors were open. Here Topper came with his leg dragging, something I hadn't noticed the night before.

He looked more handsome and more worn down than the last time we had met, and he didn't look as if he would resort to a kitchen knife if we got into a dispute about the Peace of Westphalia or the proper way to poach eggs in apple cider vinegar. He wore a tracksuit, though, and it made him look more suspicious than he needed to.

"I see you had a good sleep," I said, and he didn't say anything when I offered him coffee.

"I sleep the same every night."

"I'll bet you do. It's strange to see you in the morning light. You look almost normal."

"So do you. Are you buying me breakfast?"

"It's all ordered. This is a nice place to talk, isn't it?"

He looked around the square and the dark-red domes of the church next to us.

"It's a helluva country, all right."

I asked him where he was from. California, of course.

"We must be distant relatives, then. Are you still working for Donald? I wish I could talk you out of it."

He shrugged. I thought for a second that he was trying to smile but couldn't, and that was an interesting dilemma for a man's face.

"Maybe I am, maybe I'm not. Feels like in this country everyone's out for himself."

"That they are, cowboy."

"I like the way they do their eggs, though."

"Would you like a shot of brandy?"

He accepted and the ice seemed then to thaw between us. I reached down and placed the suitcase by his legs. I explained that I had an idea. I'd give him half the money and he would forget me and go his own way. On top of that, he would tell me more about his employers. It was a reasonable proposition, I said. He got a reasonable payoff and I got to be left alone. I wasn't out for money anyway. I just wanted to know where the Linders were headed next.

He looked at me in astonishment.

"You're *giving* me the money?"

"It's the easiest way out for me," I said. "She paid me off, and now I'm paying you off. It's worth it to me. I think you should take it and then we should go our separate ways. What do you say? I'd say that was a fair deal for you. You can go to Acapulco and waste some more of your life. You can do whatever you want. Just leave me alone and pretend you never saw me. I have a feeling you're not working for them now."

"You got me there."

He reached down and tested the weight of the suitcase.

"You just made a small fortune over breakfast," I said cheerfully. "Shall we call it a deal?"

He reached into his tracksuit pocket, took out his little top, and spun it on the tabletop while the waiters watched us. He spun it three times and then said, "All right, you got a deal."

"But I want to ask a few questions first."

I asked him if he had known the real Paul Linder. He shook his head and his little pale eyes regained their husky vigor for some reason. He had worked on the yacht the Zinns once owned and he had been in Caleta de Campos on that day. They had sold it in Panama and all the evidence of what had happened there had therefore passed into unknown hands. But what had happened? Topper ate his eggs with a single fork, and I saw that his whole good arm shook a little while the hand in the sling was clenched tight. He had been on board that night, he said, but had been sleeping. The other crewmen had told him that there had been a lot of drinking late at night and the bosses had been abusive to the employees. I asked him if he had helped take Linder's body onto the beach. He pocketed the top again, smiled, and lifted a finger: I was not to ask about things like that. He hadn't seen anything. I said that he didn't have to tell me if he didn't want to. It was just that I'd heard Donald was a sadist of sorts and apt to his lose his temper, if not his mind, at the slightest provocation.

"So I think of his wife as an abused woman. Would you say that was accurate?"

"What's it to you?"

"It's not much, but I'm interested to know all the same."

"It's not far off. We were all hired in Mazatlán that summer, three of us, and we had to take an oath of secrecy. He was Donald back then, before he became Paul, but we were all told it was because of tax and the feds. We were offered shares of the profits, so we didn't mind. I suppose you want to know why I changed my mind?"

"I couldn't care less, but tell me anyway."

"Well, if you feel that way about it I'll keep it to myself. Let's just say Donald is not only a thieving bastard but nasty to his wife. You can't stay with him forever and I don't think she will. I saw him hit her a few times. You know how those ones are. If he hits his woman, he'll do worse to his underlings. Sooner or later he stabs you in the dorsal. He finds new people as he goes along because he has the money. But no one stays for long. By the way, what happened before—it wasn't my idea, of course. I know you know that. It was a stupid idea to begin with."

"Whose idea was it?"

"I'll let you find that out for yourself. It hardly matters now anyway." He glanced down at his watch and his eyes went shifty and scattershot. "I should probably be going. I suppose I should thank you—it turned out better than I expected."

"It's filthy lucre and bad luck, but enjoy it."

What he couldn't understand, he added, was that information seemed more valuable to me than hard cash. It didn't make any sense at all, but why should he care if it made any sense or not?

"That's it, Einstein," I said. "You don't have to care. But I had one last question."

I said that I wanted to know where the couple would head if and when they took off from Guanajuato. They wouldn't be on the road as wealthy vagrants forever. They had to be heading somewhere, a place where they could settle down. Didn't he know?

"Those two? Who could say. They're gypsies. They've always been a con team together—it's all a facade. It's not really a marriage. So I think they'll just keep rolling from con to con. That's how it is with them. They just want to have fun and not have to pay for it. They're drifters."

"I can't believe it's as childish as that."

"It's not my hell, Señor. I'd rather take the dollars and head for the exit down that street. It's been very nice having breakfast with you. But if you wanted to look for them after today, or after tomorrow, I would go down to Mexico City. They can lie low in a big city much more easily and there's a hotel that Donald loves called the Gran Hotel Ciudad de México. Why you'd want to run into them again, I can't imagine. It wouldn't be what I would do."

"Maybe not."

There was something that stuck in my craw. It was un-finished business, and my guest wouldn't understand it in a million years.

"I'll sleep on it," I said. "If I'm feeling unlucky I'll go and pay them a visit."

He got up and I knew that I would never see him again, this man whom I had shored against my ruins.

"If you see them," he said before melting away, "tell him from me that his money has malaria on it but I like it anyway. He'll probably offer to pay you to kill me. *Hasta la muerte, pendejo.*"

I finished my breakfast alone and then walked back to the hotel in a much better mood. In the evening the tailored suits I had ordered were ready and I wore one of them to a little restaurant at the end of the street, where I eventually played checkers with the owner and offered him a Cohiba that I had bought earlier in the day.

For the first time in years, I felt that I was on vacation and that I had made no decisions about what I would do when my eyes opened the following day. There are times to run and there are times to pursue. Every animal knows the difference and when the moment comes to do one or the other. I found myself alone in the streets with the caped troubadours and their mandolins. Wandering, wandering, and mumbling the words *camino, camino.* The young looked at me the way you would a piece of cardboard tossed down a street on the wind. Wreckage with eyes and a pulse. The wounded animal drag-ging itself back to a tree it knows, a patch of shade where it can die in peace. The hotel stairs seemed to go up and up for miles; a hand made of wax guided me by tracing a line on the filthy wall. Was I drunk again? My dreams were of ships in gales, decks swept by relentless waves, and the threat of being lost at sea. Waters rushed past me and the ship heaved and sank; the bottom of the ocean clamored with falling coins, glasses and sextants, and cocktail shakers. And there I drifted down among them until I came to rest upon a vast bed of silver sand and fell asleep like a capsized bosun filled with water and salt.

TWENTY-THREE

I N THE EVENT, WHEN I DID OPEN MY EYES, I KNEW AC-
tually what to do. I shaved in the bedroom mirror immediately after rising, dressed in the lighter summer suit, and
then went down to the lobby to settle up and get a coffee in
the street. I had packed the small shoulder bag with my other
suit and toiletries, and I left nothing behind in the Cantarranas. No one had noticed me arriving or leaving. I, too, was
becoming a *fantasma*.

The sun had only been up for half an hour when I drove
out of the city in a taxi and made my way back to the Linder
mansion in the hills. This time I asked the driver to let me out
at the bottom of the hill where the villa stood. In the woods,
the cuckoos were roused and there was a faint and menacing
hum of bees massing in the glades. As I walked slowly up the
hill, I saw now that the villa was concealed behind tall trees
on all sides. I rang the bell at the gate, but no one stirred and
I noticed that the gate itself was not closed.

More than that, it was clear that the villa itself was deserted. I called out just in case, but I already knew that no
one, not even a servant, would come running. The lawns
were dotted with discarded bottles, and inside the porch was
a sleeping cat that had probably been there long before the

Americans arrived. I entered the house. The fittings were exactly as they had been before. So the rental had been furnished, complete with gilded mirrors and kilims. I came to the same stairwell that I had ascended a few nights earlier and looked up into its dusty gloom. The vagrants had simply waltzed out of town with their bags.

I sat on one of the steps and smoked for a while to think it over. Topper was probably correct: they had decamped to the big city thinking that no one would follow them now. It was flattering to think that it was all because of me, but I was following them now purely for the sake of pride. The worst of all human motives.

I wandered upstairs and to the same corridor that I had stumbled down that night. The doors along the corridor were all still open and the rooms filled with glasses from the party. It was as if they had simply woken up, packed lightly, and walked out of the house without a second thought. I went into the room in which they had been arguing; sheets were twisted across the floor and half-burned cigarettes scattered everywhere. I sat on their wide marital bed in the half-light of the drawn shutters and soon began to hear the birds outside in the garden sounding as if they had been excited by something. I tried to imagine them lying on that bed, scheming and making love, but I couldn't conjure such a tender scene. As my gaze swept around the bed, I noticed something lying between it and the wall where the windows were. I jumped with a nasty surprise, thinking for a moment that it might be something alive. But it was an unusually large sack with the neck closed by a twist of wire, and whatever was inside it was not alive.

I thought for a moment that it must be the trash, a few effects they didn't want to take along with them, but the contours were irregular and soft and I knew with a vile certainty that it was something human. I stepped back to the door and peered out into the landing, my heart racing faster than my pulse. There was no chance that anyone would come into the house now, but I thought about going back downstairs and locking the front door.

In the end I didn't. I went to the sack and kneeled by it. Some kind of atavistic instinct kicks in when you are close to another human being who is suffering or crippled. I reached out and prodded the surface of the sack and it yielded a little. My first thought was that he had done it in the end. He had killed her. But as I began to freeze with horror I found that I couldn't bring myself to untie the wire and see for myself. I was hit by a wave of nausea and went to the bathroom instead to see if there was any sign of a struggle. Sure enough, the floor was covered with dried blood, deep red over black-and-white squares, more Rothko than Pollock. In the basin lay a pair of clogged scissors with human hair trapped inside the blades.

I went back into the room and felt the first moments of a cold panic. I knew I should leave immediately, and shouldn't have come in the first place, but I could not act for some reason. Then, as I dithered, the sack itself stirred very slightly, or I thought it did, and I went to the door with sweat pouring down my neck. When I got to the stairs I saw that the cat had come indoors and stood at the foot of the stairwell, looking up at me and licking her chops. There was a sense of imminent commotion. I went down the steps and across the hall, and when I was halfway across it there was a considerable noise at the front door. People had arrived. The door swung open, and I wondered what kind of judgment would come down upon my head.

Then I thought purely of escape. I darted into one of the rooms off the hallway, closed the door behind me as quietly as I could, and found myself inside a small salon with a grill-covered window and no escape into the garden. I would have tried to hide, but they were coming through the rooms one by one, snapping open the doors. I have nothing to hide, I thought. It wasn't me and I could prove it. It was false and it wouldn't wash, but there was a certain relief in sitting calmly at a table in the middle of the room and waiting.

It was a Mexican police unit with two detectives in jeans and short leather jackets. They burst into the room and there was an outcry, the men calling up to the others, one of the detectives, the senior one, rushing down to the room and striding through the door.

He was clearly surprised to see me. An old gringo with a cane and a shoulder bag. But it was my appearance that shocked him, not the fact that I was there. So it was a tip-off.

He asked me if I spoke Spanish.

"As you can see."

He ordered the men out of the room and asked for my papers. I came out with an elaborate explanation as to why I didn't have it on me. What, he then asked, was I doing in an abandoned house?

I told the truth. I'd been at a party and I'd returned to thank the hosts.

"What hosts?"

"The Linders."

"Who are they?"

That was a long story and I didn't tell it.

"Just some Americans I met."

"Sit there and don't move."

He slammed the door shut behind him and then walked over to the table and sat opposite me.

He was a man of about forty-five, iron in the hair, small and chiseled and too fit. His name was Anguiano and I noticed that his hands were extremely clean, with perfectly cut and manicured nails. It isn't always the case. He didn't say anything for a few moments and then he crossed his legs and looked around the empty room. There was a look of faint disgust in his face.

"Did you go upstairs?" he said.

I said I'd stayed on the ground floor.

"Who is it in the sack? Do you know him?"

I asked if he'd got the pronoun correct, but he waved the question away, and now I could hear that they were poring through the whole house at a frenetic pace.

"Are you traveling alone?" he went on.

"I'm not married."

"I didn't ask you if you were married. I asked you if you were traveling alone."

"So it seems."

He then stood up, strode back to the door, and yanked it open. He shouted out into the turmoil and his team came running. He turned back and glared at me. They were taking me in and I was to do as they said. His men burst into the room and put on the cuffs. Outside in the hallway the sack had been brought down and the men stood around it holding their noses. Suspicion had fallen where it had to; the men were excitable and moralistic, as they often are. Dragged to my feet, I had the look of a criminal surprised, not agile enough to get away after using a pair of scissors to cut up another person. They hustled me outside and there were more men waiting in the road, the walkie-talkies bustling with chatter, the weapons sultry on hips. Down we went to the car, the little prison on wheels. The cat followed after us. Anguiano got into the back seat with me and we rolled off back to the city and a police station with a small room in a basement with a bed. There I was left with my shoulder bag while Anguiano went off to fill out the paperwork. I had made a mistake and yet it wasn't the first mistake I had made, nor was it a fatal error.

TWENTY-FOUR

H E CAME BACK WITH TWO COFFEES AND SO WE WERE alone together with only the sound of pigeons outside the room's lone window and a bulb suspended above the table. The mood was cool and undecided on his part. He wanted to know what the story was. To this question I answered that there was none: I knew no more about the sack in the upstairs room than he did.

"We ran a check on you, Mr. Marlowe. Were you in a place called Cuastecomates in the last few weeks?"

"I may have gone down there, yes."

"But you're not just a friend of the Linders. You're an investigator and were thrown out of the house the other night. Some people might say you bore a grudge against Mr. Linder. Was that the case?"

"I'm used to getting thrown out of villas."

It made him smile and he relaxed a little.

"Is that so? It must be a strange feeling. I've never been thrown out of a villa myself."

"You're a policeman."

"In Mexico it doesn't matter. They throw you out anyway."

He asked me why they had ejected me from the premises that night.

"Oh," I shrugged, "you know how the rich are."

"Are they rich?"

"I suppose they are."

"Were you blackmailing them for some extra cash?"

"It's a fine idea now that I think about it."

"Was it a fine idea the other night?"

"I went there with an open mind. I wanted to meet the man I was checking up on. You're right, I was after him."

It had to come out sooner or later, so better sooner, I thought. There was no harm in his knowing and it would get me off the hook more quickly.

"What were you investigating?"

He was taking notes, and so I thought I might as well give him half the truth. It would be enough for his imagination.

"Pacific Mutual?"

"It's an insurance company in San Diego."

And so on.

"But you could have been blackmailing them as soon as you found them. I think it's likely."

"You can think what you like."

He smiled again.

"All we have are thoughts, then."

"Well, we have a bit more than that. We have a body, for one thing. Do we know who it is?"

I said I'd like to know myself.

Something in the way I said it must have convinced him that I was not faking and he sighed and looked down at his hands folded together on the table. His marriage ring looked strangely austere and isolated, almost pathetic. He, too, stared at it as if it might inspire him to insight.

"It's a man. We can't say who it is because the body has been disfigured by an expert. The fingers have been filed down, as we say. And the face has been removed."

The sweat returned and my hands went cold and wet. I leaned back and all the air went out of me.

"The forensics people are looking at it now, but we don't have many forensics personnel here. We have to send for someone in Mexico City. Luckily, it's only four hours away with the new road. They'll be here tomorrow morning."

"Filed down?"

He smiled a third time.

"The fingerprints are removed. We call it filing down."

But that had to be a highly specialized job.

"To put it mildly. I've never seen one myself. As far as I can tell, it's a beautiful job. It was done by someone who knows what they're doing."

"So you can't identify him?"

"Not for a while. You seem genuinely curious. For a moment I actually believed your story. But I've heard investigators are Hollywood actors. Are you a Hollywood actor?"

"I'm Bollywood at best."

"I see. So you can sing and dance as well? I'd still like to know what you were doing at the house the other night. It seems a very reckless and strange thing for an investigator to do. Surely you'd want to follow them from a distance."

He was right, and I admitted it.

"But I wanted to see them in their element. It was just curiosity."

"Curiosity?"

"I'm a child like that. It's like wanting to torture small things."

"Is that so?"

He considered this for a while. Was I a repulsive specimen?

No love is lost between our two professions. It's perpetual war, gags, rib digging, and mockery. A chess game with penalties.

"You wanted to torture them. I can understand that. After a while you begin to hate the people you are chasing. I know that feeling. You want to destroy them and grind them into the dust. Is that how you feel? Everyone here is convinced that's the reason you cut off his face. But now that I look at you—I don't think you know how. It was done with a pair of scissors. That's a virtuoso act of surgery and I don't think you have the hands."

He had already glanced down at mine.

"But maybe you're glad you could destroy them. Is that what you were trying to do?"

"Maybe I was," I said truthfully.

It was truthful enough to change his mind.

"I see," he sighed. "And you have no idea who he is?"

"I can't imagine why they would kill someone in their own house. Maybe they had a score to settle."

"No. Settled scores don't involve facial surgery. It's not vengeance. It's concealment."

The body, then, wasn't just anybody.

I thought about the pathetic Roman. There was something sacrificial about him, and something between him and

217

Donald that had been partially submerged. An antagonism. But there was no reason to disfigure him.

"How tall is the body?" I said.

"About two meters. It's an oldish man. Maybe around seventy."

Then it was Donald, I thought. The realization came in a single moment, and I wondered if that meant everything was over and my mission finished.

He left me then, and for the rest of the day I slept on the cot while voices and footfalls echoed around me in the labyrinth of the station. It was as if they had temporarily forgotten or mislaid me.

I thought through all the possibilities and none of them were credible. I wondered where I was. Underneath the old city, in Spanish sewers and passageways, among cellars and catacombs. The air smelled slightly of sulfur. When the light began to fade in the window, they brought in a dinner of tamales and some Coke and I began to think that this wouldn't be as bad as I had imagined. Sure enough, I slept through the night without interruption. They must have been waiting for the forensics team to arrive from the capital. It wasn't until ten in the morning that Anguiano returned, this time more elegantly dressed. It was as if he had been in a meeting with people more important than he was. He had two coffees this time as well, and his mood seemed to have improved a little.

"The team is here and they are working on the body. I'm going to assume you are telling the truth when you say you have no idea who it is. All the same, you were the only person on the scene. It's difficult to make everyone believe in your ignorance. I only half believe in it myself. I think you went to the room and looked around and made sure the person in the sack was dead. That doesn't mean you killed him. There's no blood at all on your person and the operation will have caused a massive loss of blood. So you weren't there when he was killed."

"It's a brilliant conclusion."

"All right, it's not that brilliant but it's obvious enough. Still, you knew the renters of the house and you probably know where they are now. I think I have the right to ask you where they are."

I denied everything.

"But you have an idea."

I shook my head: "I have as much idea as you do. They're people who like to disappear. They may even have gone on to Panama."

After a pause, he went on: "We called your employers and your story panned out. So I have to let you go. I'm reluctant to do that, but I have no choice. You're free to leave now, in fact."

"It's a shame. I was getting used to the quiet."

Nor was it untrue. The cell was a welcome relief from the absurdity all around me.

"I don't suppose you're going to tell me where you are going next. I could have you followed, of course. I'd be within my rights. Someone lost his life."

"That he did," I said, and I saw his point. "I'll probably give up and go home."

I then asked him who had given them a tip-off that I would be at the house. But he shrugged; it was his information and not mine. It must have been someone who wanted me delayed for a couple of days, or maybe longer. It might not be a bad idea, I said, to trace that call and see who it might have been.

"Too late," he countered.

We went up into the parts of the station where sunlight and fresh air existed. It's strange how quickly you forget that the upper air exists, filled with lights, birds, dust, and the smell of cigarettes. He walked me to the front doors and we chatted about insurance frauds. They were mostly all the same, he said indifferently. Except for the ones who carved off people's faces. He gave me his card, which was optimistic of him, and suggested that I call him if I needed to. I replied that all I needed was a lift to the bus station. They would obviously find out where I was headed, but I didn't much care.

"Are you serious about going home?"

"I've given it some thought. There's an apple pie and a pipe waiting for me and early mornings on the beach. It's a fine life."

We came into the hot sun of the street and the white shirt he was wearing suddenly looked princely and impressive.

"You don't sound convinced," he smiled.

"After a while you get tired of hotel rooms. Even nice ones with carpets. They all smell the same."

"Ah, it's true."

I shook his hand and thanked him for the coffees.

"I wouldn't go to Mexico City if I were you," he said.

"I'll take that as good advice."

"Take it any way you want. But if you do go there there's a nice hotel on the Calle Uruguay. And by the way, I'm letting you keep the money on you even though I know it's not what you say it is. You can count it as a favor. I may need one from you someday."

He turned and went back into the building, and the car arrived to drive me to the bus station. Once there, I went straight to the counter and got a one-way ticket to Autobuses del Norte en DF. I was sorry to be back on a bus with the little boys putting Virgin of Guadalupe stamps on our knees as if we were all going to die on the road, but there was nothing for it. Dandelion seeds and the wind. I sat at the back with the window rolled down and counted the hours passing without even looking at the clock above the driver. It felt like vagrancy, and perhaps that was the state I had aspired to all along without being able to find it: to be a stone not just rolling but gathering moss as well.

TWENTY-FIVE

I HAD ONLY BEEN TO THE CAPITAL ONCE, TWENTY YEARS before, and that for a brief interview of an American heiress who had holed up in a hotel there to drink herself to death. I had talked her out of it, gone for a stroll around the Pyramid of the Sun, and come home to LA. No business had ever called me back and I already knew that the city of 1968 had disappeared, never to return. In those days, it had been the most beautiful city in the Americas. But decay is written into the genes of cities. I saw it now as we came into the suburbs north of Tenayuca. The stagnant rivers and the shantytowns filled with naked, winter-like trees. There were great expanses of musty scrub fringed with refrigerator shops and the skeletal frames of unfinished buildings. The rooftops were cluttered with bent crucifixes and pink and magnolia water tanks baked in the heat. I felt that I had seen them before. Perhaps I'd dreamed about them years before and they had come out of my own unconscious to meet me on the road.

I was sure, too, that I'd already seen the drab cement motels, those multitudes of pale-green and rose shacks smothered with smoke and the power stations bristling with steel pipes and thrown into a sea of lean-tos: I had seen them in nightmares. In the depths of a blasted tenement, its side ripped out, an ancient Christmas tree sat with its red baubles in a child's bedroom, the angel on the top sparkling in the midday light. Even if you thought of hell, you wouldn't be able to picture a landscape dominated by the proud banners of Union Carbide and Firestone. On the soiled streetlamps the Communist counterbanners made no difference; only the shrines glimmering under the power lines were beautiful. Herds of cows flashed past in bronze-tinted fields. We came to the Autobuses del Norte at three o'clock and I walked out into the street to hail a taxi to Calle Uruguay and the hotel of the same name. It was an old place from the time of D. H. Lawrence, dark and vertical, with a room free right at the top on the roof, and from there I could almost see the Gran Hotel Ciudad de México.

When I arrived I asked them to send up an iron and pressed my suits myself. Then I sat on the roof until nightfall watching some fireworks that had been set in motion in the main square. The day had been clear and the tip of Popo was visible against a pale sky well into the dusk. The streets were calm and almost silent except for the clacking of mechanical toy birds that the hawkers sold to tourists at the corners. I then called the Gran Hotel and asked them if I could speak to a Mrs. Linder.

The girl said, "She's out right now. Can I leave a message?"

"Did she make a reservation at the hotel restaurant?"

"No, sir."

"Is she with her husband, if I may ask?"

The girl hesitated and I saw at once that she suspected that the man Mrs. Linder was with was certainly not likely to be her husband. She said she wasn't sure, and our respective silences met in a moment of humor.

"Do you know when she's coming back to the hotel?"

The voice became sarcastic.

"We don't ask guests when they are returning to the hotel, sir."

I hung up and went back to the roof.

At that point I decided the best thing to do was walk over to the Gran Hotel and see what I could see.

It stood in one corner of the *zócalo* where the cathedral stood, and it was one of those Porfirian piles that old men love. It was such a popular spot, with its art deco interior and stained glass, that I went straight up to the terrace bar on the roof and decided to wait here for a while in the hope that my lady decided to do the same. On the square below, people were scattered over such distances that individually they looked like little flies, flies with no wings and no malicious vitality, and among them were men playing flutes while men in Mixtec feathers performed dances. It felt like a scene that I should have seen when I was a child but never did. Seven thousand feet up, the air was thin and everything in it shone with a different light. I waited there a fair while, but still Dolores didn't show up. In a city of many millions, there was little point in looking for her when I already knew she wouldn't show. I felt that there was now a connection between us, such that she might well sense that I was on her tail and could maneuver herself accordingly.

But hotels have ears. The ears are called waiters and bellboys.

The boy serving tables on the terrace, for a quiet tip, advised me that Mrs. Linder came up there for breakfast very early, when no one was around.

"How long has she been here?"

"She arrived two days ago. This morning she called for a cab to take her to Tepeyac. That's what the guys downstairs said."

He explained that it was a suburb with a famous church. It was in fact the great Basilica of Our Lady of Guadalupe.

"Why would an American want to go there?" he said.

It was a good question, I said. Perhaps she was a devout Catholic. And what time had she taken her breakfast? At six thirty. I told them I'd come there the following morning at the same time.

For a moment he looked nervous, but he had taken the money. He nodded and I told him not to worry; she was an old friend.

Eventually I went for dinner back on Calle Uruguay—one of those old dusty eateries with white-sauce enchiladas suizas near the hotel—and then walked up to Garibaldi using a map that the hotel had given me. The cantinas were in full swing, the mariachi strolling the plaza for tourist coin, and in one of those dens I soon found yet another Electrucador dispensing free shots for a free shock. So I went for it—it gave me a thrill. And afterward I went amok at a place where only men were drinking upright at the bar. Tequila, not a bad drink, and a few beers thrown in between. I grow old, I grow old, I will take my tequila bold. When dawn broke, however, I was already awake and dressed for a wedding.

I walked back to the Gran Hotel and stopped first at the reception desk to inquire whether Mrs. Linder had had her breakfast yet. The girl looked up with eyes that held their own suspicions in check and deferred to a dapper old man with a cane.

"Yes, sir. She already left."

"Damn, I missed her again. Did she go to Tepeyac?"

She was surprised and her glance went to the door, where the boys stood waiting to hail taxis.

"As a matter of fact, she did. Can we call you a taxi to go there as well?"

"Why, that would be very kind of you."

"*Para servirle*. It takes about forty minutes to get there."

When I got to the door I asked them if they might happen to know where Mrs. Linder had asked to be taken in Tepeyac. It had been a religious goods store on a street called Calvario that catered to pilgrims visiting the basilica: unusual enough for the boys to remember without any hesitation at all.

TWENTY-SIX

THE DRIVER LEFT ME BY A WAX MUSEUM JUST IN FRONT of the basilica and told me how to find Calvario from there. It was a small street whose crooked and untamed trees seemed much older than the buildings behind them. In the middle of it stood a two-domed church and next to this lay a line of small shops, including a clinic and an old gate that led to the Hogar de Ancianos Santa María de Guadalupe. By it, the trees met in the middle of the road, covering it completely with shade. There was a *nevería* on the corner with bright ice-cream cones painted on its walls. Between the church and the *hogar*, meanwhile, lay the shop that corresponded to the address that the boys had written down for me. Its window was filled with votive candles, little plastic dolls of the Virgin in glittering capes, and what looked like sugar skulls. The shop had just opened and a middle-aged woman was turning on the lights inside her cavern of Catholic hope and kitsch. When I opened the door, a bell rang from deep inside the cavern of the shop. The woman looked up and I could tell that I was not in the usual run of her customers. I was suddenly sure that Dolores had been there just before me, and I decided to just ask the owner up front if that was the case.

"There was no American here," she said defiantly.

"The person who was just here—where did they go?"

"Everyone who comes here goes to the basilica afterward."

I began to notice that there were small figurines of the Virgin with scythes, female reapers that were unusual. Weren't they the figures that Dolores had described as belonging to the Santa Muerte? Little shiny statues stood in rows, skeletons in silver and gold cowls and dresses holding scythes. Some were all white, some black. A few, slightly larger, were scarlet and green and the scythes had gold blades. Around them were blue and black candles and others that were banded in seven colors. The *botánica* section, the woman explained. A collection of folk medicine and magical amulets and spell-casting perfumes. The blue candles indicated wisdom; the black ones protected against black magic. Gold was for increasing prosperity.

I showed her a photograph of Donald and she shook her head. And then it occurred to me that I had forgotten to bring one of Dolores.

"Was it a woman?"

The denial was less emphatic.

So I had my answer, and I had suddenly realized something.

"When did she leave? Was it less than ten minutes ago?"

And against her better judgment she blinked while denying it.

The glass shook as I closed the door behind me. I walked away as quickly as I could toward the basilica. Around the plaza, filled with both rubble and pilgrims, I sat there in the sun breathing in the thin air with difficulty. Dolores was almost certainly there among the crowds. I entered the church, which rose like a metal bedouin tent from the edge of the plaza opposite its sixteenth-century companion. Above the altar hung the veil in which the Indian saint Juan Diego had once gathered roses, itself imprinted with a mysterious image of the Virgin.

Under it, in an automated ritual, a conveyor belt whisked the faithful under the relic to be blessed by it. Outside, loudspeakers boomed over from the markets nearby. It washed over an army of beggars and neatly groomed peddlers of Virgin memorabilia. And I moved through this crowd, sifting slowly through the cripples and the blind until—just as I turned away from the great metal tent—I saw her making her way toward the basilica.

Dolores was dressed in black with a dark-green head scarf over her hair, low heels, and a white bag slung over her shoulder. Unaware of me or anyone around her, she walked slowly into the church and I followed her at a safe distance until she got onto the conveyor belt and was dragged slowly under the veil.

She got up at the other end and went back into the nave and knelt among the wretched of the earth before crossing herself, turning, and then going back outside into the sunshine. She walked around to the *bautisterio*, near which stood an entrance to what I thought was a large park but which I soon saw was actually a cemetery. The cemetery of Tepeyac. It was crowded, but she went into the park, along a wide path filled with hundreds of people. Soon I was following her among the ponderous stone angels and the Père Lachaise–style family tombs and *camposantos*. She made her way to a grave somewhat removed from the crowds until I was only a few tombstones away from her.

At that moment a tiny, oblong cloud unconnected to any others had appeared at the outer rim of the sun and was about to dim it. It shone like liquid silver and then, as it moved, the light decreased and her eyes moved upward and met mine. But there was no recognition. Exactly then a young man appeared as if out of nowhere, stepping up to her with the confidence of the familiar, and put his arm around her.

TWENTY-SEVEN

THEY WALKED ARM IN ARM BACK TO THE PLAZA, AND I kept them both in sight. He was a Mexican man of about thirty, well dressed and slender, a man capable of turning her into one half of a respectable couple. There was nothing remarkable about them in that respect, and despite the sudden disappointment I felt, I understood the logic. It was as if old age had finally come crashing down upon me in a square filled with penitents and cripples. I was old and they were young, and they had grace where I had none.

They parted by the edge of the square—a quick kiss—and she walked back toward the religious goods shop. She went down Calvario without a care and hailed a taxi at the corner. An hour later we were both at the Gran Hotel and I got out at the square and contrived to arrive there well after her.

I stopped first at a chocolate shop and bought a small box of nougats. The boys were too busy to notice me when I came in through the lobby. I went to the reception desk and asked if I might send up the box to Mrs. Linder's room or, if they preferred, they could tell me the room number and I could take it up myself. They were flooded with new arrivals and gave me the room number purely to disburden themselves of an extra task. It was a room on the third floor. I went up straightaway and waited until the corridor on either side was empty. Then I knocked on her door.

When there was no response I considered asking one of the staff to knock for me. I wandered off until I found one of the room cleaners. Giving her the box, I asked her to take it back to the room and try again without telling the occupant who had given her the box.

She returned a few minutes later saying she had delivered the box successfully. There was a beautiful young girl in the room and she had been very surprised to be given a box of nougats.

"I'm secretly in love with her," I whispered, holding a finger over my lips and winking.

A half lie always works better than the full one.

I pictured her opening the box, seeing the wrapped squares of nougat and the note I had written in the shop. *Black Widow.*

I spent the rest of the day in my room, having already arranged with one of the doormen to call me if Dolores or her boy went out. No call came. I went up to the roof at the end of the afternoon and downed a succession of strong *caipirinhas.* My nougats had probably spooked her. Could she have guessed that her hunter was still on her heels and had broken his side of their agreement? It was now becoming even clearer that Donald had been left behind with no face in the abandoned house in Guanajuato. Had he still been with her, I would likely have left them to their devices. But it was a different tale now. Dolores had emerged into the new life she had probably been planning all along. Her motive must have been to invent a new life for herself and in this she had apparently succeeded. A new man, a new identity, her finances all lined up. Could there have been any serious reason to stay with the old man? Jealousy and hatred flashed inside me now, hatred for this new lover, for his youth, and the rage that comes with impotence. But when all that had subsided I didn't mind that, in all likelihood, he was a good-looking chucklehead and he would only get to have her for a passing season. In the end, she would shed him just as well as she had shed Donald and me. Calm down bronco, I thought. She's gone with the wind, and she likes it better that way. She, too, would grow old one day in a hidden villa with handsome servants, and I would already be dust on someone's mantelpiece.

And so the downstairs bar.

There, a large helmsman in colorful suspenders and with perfect English manned the counter. It's the one man in a hotel you can talk to. I asked him if he could make me a gimlet with Rose's lime.

"Nothing easier."

The place was deserted that night and he said a lot of guests were traveling to a place called Yautepec to visit the Carnival there and had left that night in private taxis. Some said it was the biggest Carnival in the world.

"You don't say. Where the hell is Yautepec?"

"It's to the left of a place called Tepoztlán. Don't tell me you don't know where Tepoztlán is."

"Never heard of it."

Then something occurred to me.

"Is it south or north?"

"Due south and over the mountains. About three hours if it isn't raining."

"I've always wanted to go to a Carnival. It's the one thing I never saw. I only saw them in movies."

"Don't believe anything you see in movies."

"I don't believe in anything else."

"Well, that's your funeral. Here's your gimlet."

Never did a gimlet look more beautiful, more icy green and clear.

"I'm a little *meshuga* without question," I said.

"Excuse me?"

"I'm not playing with a full deck of cards."

When I tapped a temple his eyes came alive.

"I see."

Then he laughed and rested both his hands on the counter, one on either side of the gimlet as if confronting it.

"You're a funny guy. What're you down here for?"

"What does it look like?"

"A woman?"

"What else? Maybe you saw her at the bar."

And I described Dolores.

"She's been down here a few times," he confirmed. "She only drinks soda water with grenadine."

"I suppose she was with her beau."

"Not that I saw. A bit young for you, though. I'd give that one a miss."

"When do you call it quits on that front? The madness goes on and on and then you drop dead. Hopefully anyway."

"Sure, it's better that way. She's probably down here for the Carnival at this time of year; most people are."

I ordered a second gimlet and asked him to make the lime

a little weaker. *Tepoztlán, Yautepec.* I would be throwing myself into the dark and it was a wonderful prospect.

"Then when is the Carnival?" I said.

"Tomorrow. You should go. You may not find your girl, but you'll have a good time."

I went back to my room half-snockered and called my employers. We hadn't spoken in a while and I was due to deliver an update before their patience gave out and my fee with it. I had rehearsed my little speech quite thoroughly two nights before and now it came out with a convincing ring. I explained with cold attention to detail how Zinn had been killed in Guanajuato and how thereafter the trail had gone cold. I explained the whole thing from beginning to end, a long monologue. They sat through it patiently. The money had disappeared, the principal plotter was in hell, and I was alone in a hotel in Mexico with nothing more to do. I wanted to go home.

"But what about the wife?" one of them burst out.

"She has vanished into thin air. It's her country, of course. Maybe she has the money or maybe she doesn't. I'm at a loss to know either way. I feel like I've done as much as I can. I am going to ask the Mexican police to forward their own report and you can see for yourselves. I'm sorry I never got to the bottom of it for you. *C'est la vie,* as they say in Mexico. That's French, if you didn't know."

"They don't speak French in Mexico."

"Don't they? Ah, well. I'll be damned. I've been speaking it all the time and everyone's happy. It's all the same to me. Aside from that, I'll be coming home tomorrow."

"And you didn't find any trace of our money?"

"Money's such a slippery thing, isn't it?"

"Is that a no?"

"Not a single note. It's a tragic end to a happy vacation, but we'll all survive to fight again another day. I'm finished. Would you like a receipt?"

TWENTY-EIGHT

WHEN THE ROAD TO TEPOZTLÁN DIPPED DOWN ON the mountains' far side on the road to Cuernavaca, the rain stopped and I arrived at a colonial town in a valley shadowed by sheer hillsides and karsts covered with cream-flowered shaving brush trees. It was midday and the peaks were submerged in operatic mists. I walked by myself into the town center with my shoulder bag, the streets surrounded by gardens with dark volcanic walls and the sound of human voices dominant. Once again, they were speaking Nahua. I found the *posada*, where they had a room for me. It was an old villa with liver-colored walls and rooms set around a ground-floor terrace; the owner was a woman of opulent dimensions and the dark-green eyes of Iberia. Casually, I asked about the Carnival and about the other guests. Was it a famous Carnival and so was the hotel full?

It was, she admitted, but only for the Carnival days. Everyone was headed to Yaupetec in the afternoons. Would I care to book my group taxi now?

"I am waiting for a friend to arrive from the capital. Perhaps you could check to see if she has arrived yet. Mrs. Linder."

She looked through the book without much haste and didn't see the name.

"Does she go by another name?"

I tried Dolores, Araya, and the two combined. Nothing.

"I see. She's a woman of about thirty—"

And I described her.

"Unfortunately the guests don't describe themselves before they arrive. Maybe she's coming down with a married man and doesn't want it to be known. Or are *you* the married man?"

"A ring has never darkened my finger," I lied.

"I'm sure it's not true. Such a handsome man all the same—"

For a moment old quicksilver dashed through the veins, but almost as soon as it did it came to a halt again. A sudden wind whipping through a ruin, ruffling the dust.

"But meanwhile," she went on, "I can let you know when someone like that arrives. Would you like me to do that discreetly?"

"You read my mind!"

"You don't run a hotel for twenty years without being a mind reader."

"It must be the least of your talents."

I went up to the room and lay in a bed with draped mosquito nets. The time has passed, I thought, and all that's left is empty plates. But couldn't the last days also be the time of Carnivals? Carnivals were where old men could shine a little behind their masks and pretend that their vital spirits still worked. By nightfall, fires had started up in the wide cement square in front of the church, and I went out in my crumpled panama to take a stroll. Zapatista protesters were standing around their bonfires, and the walls were covered with their red graffiti. *Traidores fuera!* But who were the traitors? High on the sierra above the town the white pyramid of the ancestors could still be seen. The seat of the pulque god "two-rabbit" Tepoztecatl, god of alcohol and drunkenness. It was a fine divinity to have looking down on me as I sat down in the square and enjoyed the protests with a cactus ice cream. It occurred to me that the revolution had finally begun after all those years. Maybe I had been waiting for it all my life. A revolution, a Carnival, whatever it might be called when all the fireworks go off and the dancing begins. A disorder of the heart that makes the coda the highlight of the song. I had already decided that after the following day, tonight was my last night. Tomorrow I would finally pack my bags and go home. I would head back to La Misión with a mind ready for fishing and naps. And tequila. I went into a cantina by the square, a hellhole filled with farmers whose eyes had already wandered off into another world. There would be no song left to sing after midnight.

They say you are never old in your dreams. You stay young and dressed as you were when you were thirty, the high noon of your appeal. At night they all come back, the clients I once had in their magnificent houses just as they were in 1940 or 1952. The whiskey flows, the banter is sharp and sexually compressed, and sunlight pours over majestic lawns and driveways. They have no idea who I am and they care even less. For them I am garbage, a paid executioner. But the women among them feel their insides move. It's the way of animals and drunks; at high noon everything looks beautiful and new.

Past midnight, I could hardly stand and a boy from one

of the cantinas escorted me home. We sang a song together
on the way and he told me that I wasn't the drunkest drunk
he had come across that week. He took me up to my room
and left me dark of mind on the bed. I lay there all night
in my clothes and dreamt that I was searching for my own
tomb in a refugee camp in a forest. The tombs were made of
wood and shaped like sleds, their outsides painted brightly.
Briefly I woke and thought I heard gunshots from the town—
either that or the Zapatistas had contented themselves with
firecrackers. I couldn't remember where I had been the evening before or what I had done. Cactus ice cream, I thought,
and that was all I thought. It rained all night. The ghosts
came into the garden and spoke in half a dozen languages.
Topsy Perlstein came speaking Nahua and dancing the can-
can. Far out in the darkness nightclubs from the past blared
their horns and for a while I could hear the sounds of Coney
Island rides.

In the morning the owner made me breakfast on the terrace. She told me that late in the night someone of Dolores's
description had arrived at the hotel and taken a room on the
ground floor, but that she had left early for Yautepec. I asked
what the name had been.

"Zinn."

"That's quite a name," I said.

"She can have whatever name she likes. It's a free country."

It was still raining, but lightly now. Thunder simmered on
the horizon. On the slopes near the hotel stood strange des-
iccated trees with dark-red coin-size seedpods hanging from

the branches while izote flowers had burst into life as if over-night. *The poetry of the earth is never dead.*

Yautepec was an hour away. It seemed to be lost among endless valleys, like a place that has been mislaid by genera-tions of madmen, and getting there was like riding on a fair-ground machine, the road rising and dipping and turning the stomach. It will be the last place I'll ever go, I kept thinking. But I'd go to get a last view of the eyes I liked so much. Yaute-pec would be the last destination in which to find a criminal. On a field just outside its center, a thirty-foot-high pole had been erected for the ritual of the flying dancers who, with whistles between their teeth, rotated around the poles on col-ored ropes. These *voladores* had already started, and so I got out there and watched the flyers whirling around the pole on their ropes while a fifth dancer sat on the pole and hit a small drum.

I walked through the town in my straw hat with a flower in its band, a bottle of tequila in hand, in the vast confusion of the chinelos, with the rain thundering down around me. The costumed brass bands and the men in brocaded hats shaped like inverted pyramids. I felt at home. Why shouldn't I have felt at home, since when all is said and done I don't have one? There are men with homes and men without them. The latter are the diviners and madmen. And now I was surrounded by hundreds of masks that imitated the long-nosed faces and curled beards of the conquerors of centuries ago, of the men who looked like me. A thousand replications of my own face. They gyrated by shuffling and jerking their shoulders so that the cascades of beads and fringes and false pearls shook up and down in a sexual motion and eventually I was dancing among them, holding my cane in one hand, abandoned and freed, and as uncool and uncalculating as my prior life had been cool and calculating. I watched as dogs dragged small clusters of intestines through the mud from the market nearby and boys with axes hauled blocks of ice through the rain. But soon the skies cleared; the afternoon was bathed in a returning heat and a soaring sun. In the covered market where the exhausted revelers recovered at the tables of cantinas and restaurants, they were butchering pigs. Day turned to night while I sat there and the Carnival became an episode from the distant past. I was alone at the end of the road and there would be no more labyrinths, and I was perfectly happy among strangers. I had always been amid strangers, anyway, moving among them with a few quips and never really arousing their respect.

As night came down I walked out to the canal or stream that ran past the market, its high banks covered with broken glass. People had passed out in the street and lay there looking up at the sky without any visible regrets. The street curved alongside the embankment and its surface was wet. I tapped my way along it until the noise had receded a bit. Eventually I sat on the embankment amid confetti that plastered the road along with crushed piñatas. I thought I could see a Ferris wheel in the distance, all the locals in Stetsons with their girls standing about in the radiance of its lights. If it didn't exist it was all the same to me. Cries and music, girls being whisked around in the Ferris wheel chairs. The confetti looked like snow, the dogs with guts in their jaws like swift reptiles. I set my now-empty bottle of tequila down in the grass next to me.

Across the street there was a bar of some kind. The plastic tables spilled into the road and under the string of bulbs a single woman sat in costume, drinking a bottle of Fanta. She wore a purple robe with silver hems and her hat was covered with sequins and tassels. She looked like a functionary of the Persian Empire in the time of Khusrow. The mask she wore was bright pink, a man's face with a gold beard and black-rimmed eyes. She looked over at me and I had the feeling that she was smiling at me. Just then I thought of the words that had been running through my head for years like mental waste but which now served a purpose. *My men, like satyrs grazing on the lawns, shall with their goat feet dance the antic hay.*

She raised the beard of the mask and slipped the whole thing upward over her head until her face came into the bar's lights. It was Dolores, the sorrowful one, and it was true that she had spotted me sitting on the bank.

She lifted the bottle of Fanta and the smile was as brilliantly unexpected as it was familiar. I had no cup to lift in her direction, but I smiled back and for a moment it was as if nothing had happened over the previous days. She pulled her mask back down, walked out into the street, and turned into the market, where the crowd was dancing. For a moment I thought of following her, but I no longer knew what I would be following or why.

Instead, I went to the bar and got my last drop of Sauza.

"Who was that?" I asked the man serving.

He shrugged, in the way of men who tend counters.

"Some woman from the city. They always come to the Carnival. They're attracted to the violence."

But what was the violence?

It was a joke. But at the same time I saw what he meant. Guns went off in the dark, that crisp *pop* that you never mistake for firecrackers. A point of frenzy was being reached, and you could say about such things that they are also the point of greatest contentment. I wanted to ask him what I should do next at my age—walk out into the fields and dance with the rest of them? But his eyes told me what I needed to know and I agreed with the plan. I got up without paying—he didn't even raise a hand—and wandered into the music and the detonating handguns. I wanted to waltz quietly with someone beautiful, but although I looked for her I couldn't find her in the melee. Later, in any case, when I was sober, I tried to remember whether I had seen even her face somewhere before in an earlier time. Somewhere at the bottom of a well, in a cinema long ago where a film was playing that no one now remembers. There have been so many of those faces and I never got the opportunity to see them age. That was the greatest sorrow of all, I suppose. I shouldn't have been in such a hurry.

EPILOGUE

I N EL CENTRO, A MONTH LATER, A SANDSTORM WAS blowing by five in the afternoon and the streets were reduced to a brown haze. The Kon Tiki's neons were turned off for the day and the Chinese owners seemed not to recognize me. I took the same room, however, and by the time I lay down it was almost dark outside. Sand hissed against the windows and spilled under the door into the room. Once again I heard the daughter practicing her violin on the ground floor and once again I agreed to meet Bonhoeffer at the diner on Adams Avenue. It was dark by the time I got there and the place was empty. He sat hunched by the window, bathed in pale-green light from the outside neon, and looked rested and splendidly indifferent to the vagaries of his own job. He had already ordered a milk shake and was doing a newspaper crossword as he sucked on the strawberry-striped straw.

He was the same as always, like something crab-like that will endure unchanged until a moment of sudden extinction. He looked up mildly and all the humor and sarcasm of those murky eyes was ready to roll into action.

"So you're back." He pumped the straw into the milk shake and then let it float. "Did you have a nice vacation?"

"I didn't get any scars, if that's what you mean. Well, maybe one or two. Mexico City was better than last time."

"Oh? I thought it was drowning in smog."

"It might be. But smog isn't the worst thing in life. Come to think of it, though, I didn't see any smog at all. It was like Virginia in spring."

"Never been to Virginia," he said.

I sat and he put down the crossword.

"Let's have two Roadkill Burgers," he went on. "It's not really roadkill. Just tastes like it."

"Roadkill's all right with me."

We both got a round of Coors and an ice bucket to go with them.

"Hell of a storm," he said, as we looked forlornly into the howling sand.

"Wasn't it storming sand last time I was here?" I said.

"It certainly was. It's like locusts. You bring it with you."

"I'm a hell of a visitor to my own country."

He tipped the edge of the hat he was still wearing.

The burgers came with paper tubs of coleslaw, pickles, and cheese fries. In the green light we looked like two aging chimps eating scraps in a cave. Along the street came rusted Mexican pickups with shadowy occupants scanning the street, the lit-up window that framed the two gringos with their cheese fries and beers.

"I've been busy since you left," Bonhoeffer said. "Though we never identified the ashes. I recorded it as an anonymous death, remains unidentified. It was the best I could do. But I have the address of the man you asked me to give them to, Linder senior. I have it here."

He pushed a piece of office paper across the table.

"You could go have a talk with him. He probably ain't the easiest."

"It's a nice thing that you did, Mr. Bonhoeffer."

"Anything to help a man back from the dead."

I took the paper and read the address: Horseshoe Lane, Glamis.

"It's on the far side of the lake in open desert, as you know. We tracked him down and it seems he's a caretaker at a gated community nearby. Or was. The community center said he retired two years ago," Bonhoeffer explained.

"Is he married?"

"No idea. He doesn't have a telephone. Hard to be married without one, I'd say."

"A loner on his own. That'll be fun."

"I'd go about it carefully if I were you. Loners have bad tempers."

"I should know," I sighed.

"Take him a bottle of whiskey. It might soften him up."

"It might soften us both up."

We ate in silence for a while and I couldn't help looking out into the empty street. I hated El Centro, but I wasn't sure I knew every reason for why I hated it. There were too many. But hadn't I liked it before? I couldn't remember.

"What if I didn't solve anything in the end? It was a trail that went nowhere. Just clues that led to other clues and then faded away. But I made enough money to buy a small boat. That's the one good thing that came out of it."

"A boat?"

"A small catamaran. I bought it outright from a guy I

know in Popotla. Now I can go fishing in my spare time. I'll probably die out there, of course. Like in *The Old Man and the Sea.*"

"More than likely."

Then he rubbed his eyes and asked me about the man out in the desert.

"That'll be my closure," I said.

"You can't know what he'll say, however."

I thought about that lobster hole I knew called Popotla. There was an abandoned arch by the road, a home furnishing business set up by the peasants nearby. That would be my place from now on. Just behind the surf, in view of Popotla teenagers selling their plaster Virgins and cattle skulls, there among them would be me, seated at my usual place, eating small tortillas, watching both them and the scarlet rock pools at the bottom of the cliffs. I'd read through the *Baja Sun* until it was time for a sundowner. On and on until the big sleep.

But meanwhile I considered that Bonhoeffer was right and I thought about it when I was back at the Kon Tiki, speculating as to how I was going to drive out in the morning to the Glamis hot springs on the far side of the Salton Sea. There was a Horseshoe Lane and he lived somewhere on it, within walking distance of the Glamis North Hot Spring Resort. It was a corner of the desert I didn't know, one of those unincorporated encampments where loners and dropouts went to escape the things they hated about our beautiful way of life.

The next day I got to the sea at about seven. The day was nothing like the previous evening. The brightness had returned. I had a coffee and doughnut in Niland and bought a bottle of whiskey for the road. In the passenger seat beside me, I placed a small suitcase filled with what remained of Dolores's money. Then I drove out to look at the long canal that cuts north–south through the desert. It's one of the strangest things you can ponder there.

The canal went directly from Slab City all the way to Glamis, and I drove alongside it with the mountains to my right and the sea to my left. The smattering of shacks and trailers on the way, with bits and pieces of hippy art cowering among the mesquites, made me wonder if old Linder came down here for his Saturday nights. Glamis had to be even more godforsaken.

So it turned out. A place with roads with names like Gas Line and System and—incredibly—Spa. It looked at first like an industrial installation or an abandoned air force base, aquafarms spread out to the left of the road, and the badlands rising up beyond the canal and Gas Line Road into peaks the color of milk chocolate.

There were only about three or four roads in Glamis, and Horseshoe Lane was easy to find. It indeed curved like a horseshoe, and within it was a trailer park with eight or nine vehicles parked behind low bushes. I left the car under a few palms on the far side of the dirt road and walked across into the trailer park. In reality, it was just a handful of trailers and a small outhouse. The wind blew hot off the mountains; small desert-willows posted by the road hissed as they were battered and the dust came and went.

Two children were playing ball on the road and I asked them where Linder lived. They pointed to a trailer that over-looked the scenery. But, they said, old man Linder was down by the canal. You could see him if you looked hard enough.

"What's he doing down there?"

"He goes fishing every morning."

"There's fish in the Coachella?"

"No, sir."

I looked down toward the Coachella Road. It was open desert between here and there, and sure enough there was a tiny human figure motionless by the canal.

I waved from the road, but he wouldn't have been able to see me. There was nothing for it but to walk down there myself, taking the suitcase and the bottle of whiskey with two paper cups.

I struck out over the burning gray sand where fan palms and creosotes stood curiously dark against a shrill sky. The tiny blue flowers of the smoke trees had begun to burst forth. A track went down to the canal, and near where it petered out over the dark-green water, an old man sat in overalls maintaining an ancient fishing rod and a line that disappeared into the scum-rimmed depths below.

He must have heard me, because his head was already half-turned, and he watched me from the corner of one eye. He was a desert gnome made of wire and thorns, a human tumbleweed in a plaid shirt, with a can of tobacco and a pipe laid in the sand beside him. I decided the best thing would be to sit down next to him after asking permission.

"Got a problem with your leg?" he said as my shadow fell against him.

"I'm getting on all right."

"You from El Centro?"

"Not really. But I was there last night."

"So what's in that suitcase?"

"Candies."

He smiled and turned back to the green water. The sun fell harshly into his eyes, but they didn't flinch.

"Then I know why you're here."

"I'm not hiding it," I said. "Would you like a drink?"

He looked at the label of the bottle I had brought. Mars Single Malt.

"What in hell is that?"

"It's Japanese whiskey. A friend sends it to me from Yokohama."

"I'll be damned."

"Is that a yes?"

"Sure in hell it's a yes."

I poured and it was pax between two old men.

When he had sipped it, he rolled his eyes.

"Damn, that's good. Better than Famous Grouse."

"Is that what you drink here, Famous Grouse?"

"In Niland where's you can get it."

"Well, *banzai* and all that."

"Funny thing," he said, "I was at the Battle of Midway, back in '42."

"Then double *banzai* to you, old-timer," I said, raising my cup.

"Thanks for the drink. You already know my name, I reckon. And yours?"

I told him and he took a second, longer sip.

"I want to know about the ashes," I said.

"I don't know much about it. I went down to collect them when word got around that Paul had died in Mexico. I had a feeling the night before he went off. He said he was going to work on a yacht for his boss. They had come out looking for people to man the yacht. They wanted down-and-outers."

"A strange thing to want."

"No, not strange. The bosses are like that. They want people who'll keep quiet and do what they're told. Who'll disappear afterward and who'll do anything they ask. It's not strange."

"But he hadn't gone before."

"Maybe he had. He never told me. But that time he went and it was good money. He went and never came back."

"I came here because—well, I wanted to say sorry."

"What for?"

"For not finding him."

He looked at me with complete coldness.

"Were you looking for him?"

"In a way I was. I did find his money, though. I figured it was yours."

I set the suitcase down next to him, but he didn't look at it.

"I was asleep in my trailer," he continued, "and I woke up and I saw my long-dead father came to me and told me he was dead, and that they were going to cremate him in the morning. That's what he told me. So I got dressed and drove down to the police station in El Centro and asked them where the cremation was happening. And sure enough, the old man didn't lie to me. It wasn't a dream."

"Did you take the ashes?"

"They let me take them. I couldn't prove nothing. But they let me take them."

"Where are they now?"

He lifted his eyes to the blue haze of the smoke trees in

the middle distance. Cholla cactus shimmered gold around them.

"I took him out there," he said, pointing to the desert. "It seemed the best."

I emptied the cup and filled it again. We drank for a while without a further word and I let the sun penetrate deep into my chest. So I had been in the wrong place all along. Far out in the plain that rose toward the candy-colored mountains a dust twister rose up and moved against the light like something seen by Ezekiel, and for all I knew it could have been his ashes disturbed by a movement from the spirit world. Then the dust settled and we sat there for a long time, declining to disturb the moment or to add a single word to what had already been left unsaid.

AUTHOR'S NOTE

TO STEP INTO the mind of another writer is always a perilous presumption, but perhaps not as perilous as stepping into the mind of one of his characters. Nevertheless, I have tried to stay within the bounds of Marlowe's fictional biography. His date of birth was always vague. As Bill Henkin, the Chandler scholar, once wrote, Marlowe had been born in "that time out of time that allowed him to be thirty-three in 1933, forty-two in 1953, and forty-three and a half in 1958." In a letter of 1951, Chandler himself put his detective's age as thirty-eight. This yields a presumptive date of birth anywhere between 1903 (since *The Big Sleep* was set in 1936) and 1915. I have opted to assume the latest of these possible birth dates, then added a year for the sake of poetic license.

I hardly need mention that many later reincarnations of the Marlowe character—for example, Robert Altman's 1973 version of Marlowe in *The Long Goodbye*—were the result of even greater licenses being taken. Elliott Gould in Altman's masterpiece is a man in his thirties rolling through 1970s Hollywood and Mexico. It was only after I had finished this manuscript, incidentally, that I realized that Altman also ends his interpretation of that novel on the streets of Tepoztlán—a coincidence so heavy-handed that it needs to be either disavowed or simply pointed out.

I have tried to stay faithful to the bewilderingly dreamlike plots of Chandler because it has always seemed to me that they incarnate the qualities of both fairy tale and nightmare to which he aspired. The plot of *The Big Sleep* was so occult that even William Faulkner, one of the screenwriters, was unable to follow it; and when Howard Hawks finally consulted Chandler to find out who killed the minor character Owen Taylor, the author had to admit that he himself also had no idea. And of course it doesn't matter.

As has been often pointed out, Marlowe's original name in early stories was Mallory in honor of Sir Thomas Malory, the fifteenth-century author of *Le Morte d'Arthur*. Accordingly, Marlowe always possesses the curious and melancholy purpose of a knight-errant. Yet Chandler also once wrote, in a letter to his friend Maurice Guinness, "I see Marlowe always in a lonely street, in lonely rooms, puzzled but never quite defeated." It is that single sentence, for reasons unknown, which has guided me in my own attempt to create yet another Marlowe after so many illustrious precedents. A character who is an exaggeration, as his creator used to say, of the possible.

LAWRENCE OSBORNE
Bangkok, March 2018

ACKNOWLEDGMENTS

I WOULD LIKE TO THANK Ed Victor, Graham C. Greene, and Charlotte Horton for bringing this proposition to my door. Without them, I would never have made so bold as to try to inhabit the shade of Raymond Chandler, a writer I have idolized since I was a child.

ABOUT THE AUTHOR

LAWRENCE OSBORNE was born in England but has traveled and lived all over the world. He is the author of the critically acclaimed novels *The Forgiven, The Ballad of a Small Player, Hunters in the Dark,* and *Beautiful Animals.* He is the third writer, after John Banville and Robert B. Parker, to be asked by the Raymond Chandler estate to write a new Philip Marlowe novel. In *Only to Sleep,* Osborne draws from his time working as a reporter on the Mexican border in the early 1990s. His nonfiction includes *Bangkok Days* and *The Wet and the Dry.* His short story "Volcano" was selected for *Best American Short Stories 2012,* and he has written for *The New York Times Magazine, Condé Nast Traveler, The New Yorker, Forbes, Harper's,* and other publications. He currently lives in Bangkok.